Pilot Panic!

Justin stared at the instrument panel like he'd never seen it before.

"You okay?" I asked.

He didn't answer. He gripped the control wheel so hard his knuckles went white.

Joe glanced sharply at Justin, sizing up the situation. "We need to start making the descent," he instructed.

"I know that!" Justin snapped.

But he didn't do anything. He just stared at the panel.

This guy had no idea what to do.

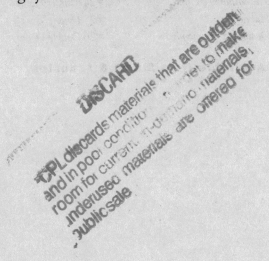

THE HARDY BOYS

Undercover Brothers®

Available from Simon & Schuster

THE

HARDY

Undercover Brothers®

BOYS

FRANKLIN W. DIXON

#26 Double Down

Aladdin Paperbacks

New York   London   Toronto   Sydney

ALADDIN PAPERBACKS
An imprint of Simon & Schuster Children's Publishing Division
1230 Avenue of the Americas, New York, NY 10020
Copyright © 2009 by Simon & Schuster, Inc.
All rights reserved, including the right of reproduction in whole or in part in any form.
THE HARDY BOYS MYSTERY STORIES is a trademark of Simon & Schuster, Inc.
ALADDIN PAPERBACKS, HARDY BOYS UNDERCOVER BROTH-ERS, and related logos are registered trademarks of Simon & Schuster, Inc.
Designed by Sammy Yuen Jr.
The text of this book was set in Aldine 401 BT.
Manufactured in the United States of America
First Aladdin Paperbacks edition December 2008
10 9 8 7
Library of Congress Control Number 2008934096
ISBN-13: 978-1-4169-7446-8
ISBN-10: 1-4169-7446-6
0412 OFF

TABLE OF CONTENTS

It's Not Over Till It's Over

Y ou probably think movie stars have it easy. Lots of money, loads of friends, 24/7 fun.

Well, okay, that's all true.

But there's a downside. Believe me. My brother Joe and I got to see that up close and personal this past week. We've been hanging with Justin Carraway. Yep. *The* Justin Carraway, Teen Movie Star. But before you get too impressed with our extreme coolness, we met Justin because of an ATAC case. See, Justin Carraway *does* have it all—including stalkers, loonies, and people wanting him dead.

That's where we came in. American Teens Against Crime—ATAC—asked us to become part of Justin's crew. He'd been getting a weirder brand of fan mail than usual. Not the usual "I love you so much, will you marry me?" type letters. These letters were threatening. And someone did try to off Justin. Turns out, a movie star can have as many enemies as he has fans.

Justin didn't exactly make it easy for us to protect him. That dude loves attention, likes to party, and doesn't want anyone telling him what he can and can't do. It's all about the fun to Justin. It took a dead paparazzo photographer and all of us nearly dying in a fire for the seriousness of the situation to register.

It was Justin's bad behavior that made him a target in the first place. The crazy letter writer was the president of a group called Cleen Teens, and they didn't approve of Justin's wild ways. Thought he was a bad influence on teens of America. I can't exactly argue with them on that point, but that doesn't give them the right to kill the guy!

Luckily, we figured out what was going on in time to keep the real bullets from being shot out of the prop gun—right into Justin's heart.

Something still nagged at me, though. That paparazzo. The Cleen Teen president—our perp—had no trouble confessing to his crimes. But he absolutely denied killing the photographer. Maybe he didn't want murder on his rap sheet; *attempted* murder was his limit. But still . . . the case didn't feel finished.

I just wasn't ready to let it go.

 JOE

Admit it, bro. You're not ready to let go of the perks that came with being in Justin's entourage.

 FRANK

That would be *you*, Joe. Yeah, sure, it was cool getting into clubs without standing in line, but—

 JOE

And the girls. Even *you* must have noticed the girls.

 FRANK

Just ignore him. I usually do.

Anyway, I was lying in bed, going over the events of the past few days, when Joe popped his head into my room, cell phone in hand.

"What's up?" I asked.

"Got a phone call," Joe said, flopping onto a chair. "From Rick Ortiz."

"The production assistant from Justin's film?" I asked. "What did he want?"

"Help."

I sat up, wide-awake and ready for action. "Was

Justin threatened again?" I *knew* we'd missed something when we couldn't tie the murder of the photographer to the Cleen Teen prez.

"Actually, it's Ryan," Joe said.

"Justin's brother?" Justin Carraway started in show biz as a double act—literally. Because of child labor laws, a child actor could only work very limited hours, so most TV shows and movies hired twins. One would work for a while, then the other would be swapped in. So Justin and Ryan shared the role of little Jimmy O'Hara on *Five Times Five,* an old sitcom. But as the Carraway twins got older, their longtime manager, John "Slick" Slickstein, decided that only one of them could become really successful. He decided that one was Justin.

Ryan seemed to be okay with it—he worked in his brother's company, and Justin was amazingly generous with the goodies. But still, it had to hurt to not be the chosen one. And to take orders from his own brother.

"Why does Rick need help with Ryan?" I asked.

"He can't find him," Joe replied. "Justin called Rick with his usual list of crazy requests. Rick went to Ryan's room to get some assistance, but he wasn't there. His bed hadn't even been slept in."

I frowned. "That's not like Ryan." Ryan was the responsible one in that pair.

"That's what has Rick worried."

"Do you think Ryan finally got fed up and split?" Ryan not only had to watch Justin make all kinds of messes, he had to clean them up, too. And it couldn't help that Ryan had a big crush on Emily Slater, Justin's costar. The same Emily Slater Justin had dated and dumped.

"Rick doesn't think so," Joe replied. "Ryan would have let him know. They're pretty tight."

"What did Justin say when Rick asked him about Ryan?"

"Rick hasn't told him yet," said Joe. "He was hoping maybe we knew something. Rick doesn't want to be the one to get Ryan in trouble."

I had a sudden thought. A disturbing one. "Could someone have snatched Ryan, thinking he was Justin? Those two are seriously identical."

Joe's blue eyes widened. "Oh man, I didn't think of that."

"If that's true, then Ryan is in serious danger," I said. "And Justin could be a target."

"We should get over there," Joe said. "The first twenty-four hours are crucial for clues."

We jumped into high gear. I grabbed the jeans and T-shirt I had worn yesterday and pulled on my high-tops before running out of my room.

I barreled down the hall and collided with Joe. He

was still yanking his T-shirt down over his head.

"Where's the fire?" our parrot Playback squawked from the armoire in the hall. "Where's the fire?"

"Shh," Joe told the parrot. "We don't want to stop for—"

"Breakfast, boys!" a voice called out from the kitchen.

My shoulders slumped. Aunt Trudy would never let us out of the house without a hearty—or as she jokes (lamely)—"*Hardy* breakfast."

"Can we sneak out the back?" Joe whispered.

"Where's the fire, boys?" screeched Playback. Loudly. "Where's the fire, boys?"

There are times when I think that bird wants the bad guys to win.

Just then Joe's cell phone rang again. "Rick," he announced, glancing at the phone screen. "Hey, Rick," he said into the phone. "Oh, okay. Well, that's good, then. Catch you later."

"Well?" I asked, after he flipped his phone shut.

"We can stay and have Aunt Trudy's waffles after all," he said, slipping his phone back into his pocket.

"Rick found Ryan?"

"No—he told Justin that Ryan was missing. Justin explained that Ryan went on vacation."

"Without a word to anyone?" I asked. That seemed out of character.

Joe shrugged. "Maybe Ryan didn't want anyone to talk him out of going."

"Rick would definitely have tried," I said. "Without Ryan around, he's going to have a hard time keeping Justin in check."

"No joke. He even asked if we'd be willing to keep hanging with Justin. Pitch in on the superstar errands."

"Maybe that would be a good idea," I said. "Not just to help Rick out, but—"

Now it was *my* cell phone that rang.

"My favorite all-American supercute good influence."

"Hi, Sydney," I said. Sydney Lamb was Justin's publicist. She was the one who set us up with Justin so we could find his stalker. That wasn't why she did it, of course—that was totally a secret mission. Our cover was that we were high school students (not a stretch—we *are* high school students) sent to welcome Justin to Bayport. She thought we'd provide "wholesome" photo ops for Justin, so she introduced us to him. She was always doing damage control, repairing Justin's bad-boy reputation.

Believe me, she earns every penny of her paycheck.

"So, I was wondering if you and your equally cute

brother would like to go with us when the movie moves to its next location."

"Really?" I asked. "Why?"

"Ryan took off without telling anyone," Sydney complained. "So not like him. That means other people—people like *me*—are going to have to pick up the slack. The biggest headache, of course, is keeping Justin in line. Maybe you and your brother can help me out there. I'd really love to have one day when I don't have to clean up some mess he's made all in the name of fun."

"I have a feeling that if Justin wants to do something, it will take more than Joe or me to hold him back."

Sydney sighed. "Don't I know it. But I don't know what else to do. We're moving to Atlantic City tomorrow, and there are just too many ways for him to get into trouble there. Rick will have *his* hands full without Ryan. And Justin already likes you. I can put it to him so it doesn't seem like you're there to babysit him. I can probably get you hired on as assistant PAs."

"Assistant production assistants?" I asked. "Does that job even exist?"

"It does if Justin wants it to."

"Let me run it by my brother and our parents."

"Great. Get back with good news ASAP."

I clicked off and told Joe about Sydney's request.

"Atlantic City?" Joe repeated. "Awesome! Cool casinos, fancy hotels, the beach, and all those perks that come with being around Justin. Of course we'll say yes!"

"Slow down," I said. "ATAC thinks the Justin Carraway case is closed. They could assign us something else."

Joe studied my face. "You don't believe the case is really finished, do you?"

I shook my head. "Nope. Not with a dead body unaccounted for."

"And ATAC isn't the big problem," Joe said.

"Mom and Aunt Trudy."

"Exactly. Gotta get permission."

Lady Luck

I started formulating my argument. "School's over. We got decent grades. Why would they say no?" I headed into the kitchen.

"Say no to what?" our mom asked. She and Aunt Trudy loaded waffles onto plates.

"We just got offered spots as assistants on Justin's film, *Undercover*," I said. "Actual jobs!" I thought emphasizing the summer job angle was a smart bet.

"Why would we say no?" Mom asked.

I was stunned. That couldn't have been easier. "Great!" I said. "So we should be back in about a week." I settled down at the table and speared a waffle with my fork.

"Back?" Mom repeated. "Back from where?"

Oops. I'd forgotten to mention the fact that the film was moving locations.

I looked to Frank. He was useless. He just kept his head down, meticulously pouring syrup into each waffle square. Letting me hang!

Frank is always on my case about how we need to plan, how dangerous it is to improvise, blah blah blah.

Unfortunately, this was an example that actually might prove him right.

"Oh!" I said, stalling. "The film is going to move to a new location for a few scenes."

Suddenly Frank's plate landed in his lap. He jumped up, sending the sticky mess clattering to the floor.

"Sorry, sorry, sorry!" he said. He picked up the waffle and the plate and put them on the table. "I'd better go upstairs and change." He hurried out of the room.

I've seen my brother be a dork, but I've *never* seen him clumsy. What was up with him?

The good thing about his klutziness was that it bought me a little time. I grabbed a wad of paper towels. "I'll take care of it," I told Mom and Aunt Trudy.

But by the time I wiped up the last of the maple syrup and retrieved Frank's fork from under the fridge, I still hadn't come up with anything.

It's not like we could tell Mom and Aunt T the real reason we wanted to go. I agreed with Frank: This mission wasn't over. Not until we knew for sure who had killed Elijah the photographer—and why.

But our work was a secret. Mom, Aunt Trudy, and even our best friends were clueless. Only our dad knew. He'd created ATAC after being a PI and working with the police for years. ATAC agents worked cases adults would have trouble with. Like hanging with teenage movie stars. A high school kid would be able to get a lot more information than any adult in that situation.

Just as I sat back down in my chair, and Aunt Trudy had kindly replaced my cold, hard waffle for a fresh one, Frank returned. He had changed pants and was followed by our dad.

"Sorry for being so clumsy," said Frank, settling back into his chair. "So what were we talking about? Oh yeah." He turned to Dad, who helped himself to orange juice from the fridge.

"Guess what," Frank told Dad. "Joe and I have been asked to work as assistants when Justin's film moves to Atlantic City."

Way to go, bro. Frank's close encounter of a sticky kind was no accident.

"I don't know," Mom said. "That Justin is pretty reckless. He seems to attract trouble."

"He *is* a high-spirited boy," said Aunt Trudy, but she had a twinkle in her eye.

Okay, let me just state for the record: Aunt T's crush on Justin has ick factor all over it.

"Befriending Justin while he was in town was one thing," Mom continued, "but now you want to go off to a place known for gambling—"

"And surfing!" I pointed out.

"And organized crime—"

By this time Dad had joined us at the table. He gave me and Frank a nod. "The boys are on summer vacation now," he said, reaching for the syrup.

"I don't know . . . ," said Mom.

"Atlantic City isn't far. And they'll be working the whole time."

"That's true," Mom said. I could see she was wavering.

"A job like this will look great on college applications," Frank pointed out.

My brother. He was an expert in finding the angle that would get adult approval.

"I hear there are great outlet stores," I put in for good measure. "Any requests?"

Mom laughed. "How do you know about designer discounts?"

I shrugged. "One of the girls at school was bragging about getting great bargains when she went to the Jersey shore. One of the places she mentioned was in Atlantic City."

Frank laughed. "Figures. If a girl is involved, Joe practically has a photographic memory."

I tossed a piece of bacon at him. He caught it in his mouth and grinned.

Mom sighed. "Oh, all right. You can go. Just be careful around Justin."

Of course, she had no idea that the real reason we wanted to go to Atlantic City wasn't because we wanted to hang with Justin Carraway. It was to tie up the loose ends of a murder investigation.

We just had to hope Lady Luck was on our side!

Nosedive

The next day our dad dropped us off at the Bay-port Airport.

"I understand why you don't feel you've truly completed the mission," he said. "The fact that there has still been no confession from Justin's stalker about the murdered photographer bothers you."

"It just feels wrong," I said.

"I'm proud that you want to stick with it," said Dad. "But remember, you can't always figure everything out. It's possible the perp will confess eventually. It's also possible the murder wasn't even related to Justin. Elijah wasn't exactly well liked."

True. *I* hadn't liked the pushy, sneaky photographer. But that didn't mean I wanted him dead. "But it's possible the murder *is* somehow connected to Justin," I said. "Which means he could still be in danger."

"And so could you," Dad reminded us. "Stay alert. This isn't an official ATAC assignment. You're on your own here."

"We'll be fine," Joe assured him.

"Keep me posted," said Dad. "If there are any breaks in the case, I'll let you know."

We grabbed our backpacks and headed for the section of the airport reserved for private planes. I was psyched. I love flying.

It wasn't hard to locate Justin. There was a crowd of photographers snapping pix. Sydney was gabbing on her cell while Justin chatted, smiled, and posed. I didn't see anyone else from the film, though. They must not be taking such fancy transportation.

Justin noticed us. He loped over, a huge grin on his face.

He slung an arm along our shoulders. "My new favorite peeps!"

Sydney looked surprised to see us. "What are you doing here?" she asked.

Joe and I exchanged confused looks. "Uh, you

asked us to work as assistants, since Ryan isn't around?" Joe prompted.

"I know that." She waved a gloved hand. The lady always wore gloves. Today they were shocking pink and matched the equally shocking pink thing on her head. I think it was supposed to be a hat.

"I mean, why are you here at the airport? The crew is traveling by bus."

"I invited them, that's why," Justin answered for us. "I thought it would be fun to have a coupla pals on board."

"But—," Sydney began.

"See you in Atlantic City," Justin said pointedly.

Sydney looked disappointed. "But we can all—"

"Boy time!" Justin grinned. "No girls allowed." He turned and started walking away. "So, have you ever flown in one of these babies?"

Sydney frowned, then stomped away. Justin was back to treating her like an employee. It was weird—sometimes he behaved as if he couldn't survive without her, and the next minute he was yelling at her and defying her instructions. Actually, that kind of summed up how Justin acted with everyone, even his twin Ryan. That was one of the reasons it had been hard to pin down a suspect. Justin just kept making people mad at him!

"Sweet," I said as we climbed into a beaut of a Cessna light aircraft. "Is it yours?"

"Nah, it's a rental. But if I like it enough, maybe I will buy it!"

The interior was plush. It was set up like a lounge—large leather reclining chairs, a small kitchen area, a flat-screen TV, and a DVD player. It was fancier than some living rooms I'd been in!

"Hello, boys." I turned to see the pilot stepping into the plane. "I'm Eddie. I'll be your pilot today. You must be Justin Carraway."

"That's right," Justin said. "And these are my buds, Frank and Joe Hardy."

"I heard from the pilots back in L.A. that you've been doing really well with your lessons," Eddie said. "All you need now for your certification is a few more air hours."

Justin's head ducked down, almost as if the compliment embarrassed him.

"You fly?" asked Joe. "Don't you love it? We got our licenses awhile back."

"You should be ready to shoot those scenes right on schedule," Eddie said.

"You're going to do your own flying in the film?" I asked.

"That's the plan," Justin said.

"So cool!" said Joe.

"Belts on, boys," Eddie told us. "Time to get airborne."

Eddie did a preflight check of the instruments, then got the go-ahead from the tower. Liftoff was smooth.

Once Eddie gave the go-ahead, Justin unclicked his seat belt. "I'm hungry," he said. He opened some cupboards and the fridge. Then he stared at the microwave. "Usually someone else takes care of this stuff for me," he muttered.

I got the hint. "What do you want?" I asked, unbuckling my seat belt and joining him in the galley area.

"I saw some pizzas in the freezer."

I popped the frozen pie into the microwave and punched the button. "See," I said. "Not so hard. A lot easier than flying a plane."

The microwave dinged, and I gave Justin his mini-pie. I pulled another mini-pie out of the freezer and held it up so Joe could see it. He gave me a thumbs-up, and I slipped it into the microwave. "Ever been to Atlantic City?" I asked Justin.

"Nope," he said, taking a bite of his pizza. "But I'm glad to be getting out of Bayport." He wiped cheese off his chin with his sleeve. "Nothing against your hometown, but with all that craziness last week, it's good to get away for a couple of days."

"I can see that," said Joe, coming over and hovering around the microwave.

"The best part is that Sydney lined me up a hosting gig at this big Martial Arts Expo," Justin said. "It's a great promo for *Hong Kong Challenge*."

"That's the movie that's about to premiere?" Joe asked.

"Yup!" Justin pulled a soda out of the fridge and took a swig. "You guys should come. I'll hook you up with some tickets."

"Awesome!" Joe exclaimed.

"What's it about?" I asked, getting our pizza out of the microwave.

Justin grinned. "It totally rocks. I'm a martial arts student and I have to fight all these masters. I'm after this mythical object so I can rescue my beloved teacher's beautiful daughter."

"Did you do the stunts in that one too?" I asked.

"With Ryan's help. Ryan's a black belt. I never made it that far." He laughed. "I guess I just don't have the discipline."

Justin was always willing to admit his own shortcomings. It was part of the charm factor. How could you bawl a guy out for being irresponsible when he totally owns up to it first?

"So where *is* Ryan?" Joe asked.

"He took off to the Caribbean for some R and R."

"Really?" I asked, surprised. "People don't usually go to the Caribbean this time of year. It's the beginning of hurricane season."

"That's probably why he chose it," Justin said. "Less crowded, fewer tourists. In case you haven't noticed, we tend to be surrounded."

"That's for sure," I agreed.

"Hey, Justin," Eddie called from the front seat. "Why don't you take the controls?"

Justin looked startled. "But I'm hanging with my buds," he protested.

"Come on, kid," Eddie said, standing. "Don't be shy—go ahead, clock some air time."

"I call shotgun!" Joe scrambled up to the cockpit and sat in the copilot's seat.

Justin looked nervous.

"I mean it," Eddie said. "I can't give you a go-ahead without having you log some time."

"Uh, okay." Justin got into the pilot's seat. He looked kind of white. Or maybe green. Eddie didn't seem to notice as Justin sank into the pilot's seat.

I didn't like the looks of this. Green is not the color you want to see on your pilot's face.

Eddie vanished into the bathroom. I hurried to stand behind Justin's seat.

Justin stared at the instrument panel like he'd never seen it before.

"You okay?" I asked.

He didn't answer. He gripped the control wheel so hard his knuckles went white.

Joe glanced sharply at Justin, sizing up the situation. "We need to start making the descent," he instructed.

"I know that!" Justin snapped.

But he didn't do anything. He just stared at the panel.

This guy had no idea what to do. What about those lessons? Did he hire someone else to show up in his place or something? Or was it just stage fright?

"Listen," Joe said, "Frank and I—"

The plane suddenly rattled and bounced.

"I didn't do anything!" Justin shouted.

"It's just turbulence," I said. "You feel it more in these small planes."

Before any of us could do anything, we bounced again. So hard that my head hit the roof. This time Justin let go of the control wheel and covered his eyes. The small plane lurched—and so did my stomach!

Someone had to take control of this plane. Or we weren't going to land in one piece.

Pharaoh's Delight

Turbulence doesn't scare me. A freaked-out pilot with his eyes shut does.

Something had to happen—and fast.

"Put your head between your knees!" I ordered Justin. He probably thought I was telling him to get into crash position, but I really just wanted him to get out of my way.

He did as he was told as I unbuckled my seat belt.

I had to get control of the aircraft, and I wouldn't be able to do that from the copilot's seat.

The plane was acting like a bucking bronco. Frank gripped the back of Justin's seat to stay upright. "We're going to stall," he warned.

I leaned over Justin and grabbed the control wheel. I couldn't get to the rudder pedals on the floor, so I had to figure out another way to stabilize the plane. We started to spin.

I could see the ground. First it was below me, then it was above me.

Concentrate, I told myself. *Don't let yourself get dizzy.*

Pizza crusts flew onto the control panel. Stuff was falling in the lounge area.

"We've lost lift!" Frank shouted over the banging and clanging of the plane.

"No kidding!" I shouted back.

My training kicked in. To get out of a stall, I needed to dip the nose. I pushed on the control wheel hard. The plane tilted, just as I wanted it to. I eased up just a hair, and the ground went back to where it belonged. Far below us.

Eddie suddenly appeared, looking panicked.

"What's going on?" he demanded. "I was gone five minutes, and we're upside down!"

Justin popped back up, banging into my chest, making me release the control wheel. I flopped back into the copilot's seat. The plane tilted.

"Justin," Eddie ordered. "Hands on. Now." He gripped the back of my seat. "You two. Buckle up and stay put."

I could have handled the descent, but I was glad Eddie was back in charge. Someone had to handle Justin!

Justin's hands shook as he placed them on the controls again. Once it was clear that we were cruising smoothly, Eddie ordered Justin out of the pilot chair.

Eddie sat down, and I followed Justin back to the lounge area. He quickly buckled his seat belt. Frank and I did the same. Justin looked completely shaken and embarrassed.

"What is wrong with you, Justin?" Eddie shouted from the pilot's seat. "You do not *ever* let go of the controls!"

I glanced at Justin. He slumped farther down in his seat. The Justin I knew would have exploded or mouthed off. He must have been really scared. Or really airsick.

"I—I don't know what happened," Justin said meekly. "I guess I did panic. Sorry."

The landing was smooth as cream pie, but the thing between Justin and Eddie was definitely ragged. We climbed out of the plane in silence.

"You know I'm going to have to report this incident to the other instructors," Eddie warned as he tossed our luggage onto the tarmac.

"Whatever," Justin muttered as Eddie stalked away.

An airport employee arrived and loaded our baggage into a Jeep. We slid in and drove to the terminal.

"You're going to have to let the director know you're not ready," Frank warned. "It's just too dangerous."

"Will she be mad?" I asked.

Justin shrugged. "She didn't want me to do the stunts in the first place. Neither did the producers. It's a big insurance risk for a star to do the stunts."

"Makes sense," said Frank.

"I shouldn't have insisted," Justin confessed, laughing sheepishly. "I kind of threw a tantrum about it. I guess that was a mistake."

I was impressed. Sure, on the one hand, Justin totally bailed on his promise to be up to speed with the flying after making such a stink. But he was admitting his mistake and wanted to do the responsible thing.

"Here's our ride," Justin announced.

An enormous limo was waiting at curbside, complete with a uniformed driver. The airport worker loaded our bags into the trunk as we slid into the super-plush interior.

It was a quick drive from the airport to the strip where the huge casino hotels were. I was surprised by how run-down everything looked. It looked like a high-crime area.

Then we turned onto the avenue lined by the big casinos. Night and day. These buildings were huge and shiny, with landscaped gardens, gigantic sculptures, or fountains.

My eyes nearly bugged when the driver went up a winding lane to what looked like a ginormous pyramid. It was painted gold, and desert-type plants lined the driveway. We pulled up to the hotel entrance and came to a stop. The driver got out and began unloading our bags.

"Where is everybody?" Justin fumed.

"Everybody who?" I asked.

"We probably arrived before Sydney and Rick, since they were driving," said Frank.

"Where are the photographers?" Justin griped as he climbed out of the limo. "The hotel greeters! Are we supposed to just carry our bags in ourselves?"

"No problem," I said, quickly picking up my backpack from where the driver had unloaded it. "We hardly have anyth—"

"Drop it," Justin ordered.

I dropped it.

"This is ridiculous!" Justin paced in a circle.

This was the Justin I knew.

"Maybe Sydney wanted to keep your arrival quiet," Frank offered. "After everything that happened last week. No paparazzi, no crazed fans."

Justin's jaw set.

"Come on," I said, picking up Justin's bags. "Let's just get inside. There will probably be loads of people waiting to meet you in there."

"Fine." Justin stalked into the hotel.

"Looks like someone needs an attention fix," I said to Frank as we followed Justin inside.

Justin stopped in the middle of the soaring lobby. The walls were covered with hieroglyphics, and tall columns were painted gold and blue. It was pretty impressive, though I wasn't sure why someone would want to stay in a dead king's tomb.

Justin didn't take in the cool surroundings; he just crossed his arms and glared.

We have tough missions for ATAC. Believe me. But dealing with a demanding movie star might turn out to be our toughest assignment ever. I wished Sydney or Rick were with us.

"He looks ready to go ballistic. We'd better get him to his room, fast," Frank said quietly.

"I'm on it," I said. "You stay with Justin and try to keep him from creating a scene."

"Sure, give *me* the hard job," Frank muttered as I dropped one of Justin's suitcases and my backpack at his feet. I went off to figure out how to get us to our rooms.

Over to the side, I spotted a group of college-age

girls. Jackpot. I sidled up near them and pulled out my cell. "You won't believe who is standing in the lobby right now!" I said loudly into my phone. *"Justin Carraway."*

The girls scanned the area immediately. When they spotted Justin, they chattered furiously and at an even higher pitch. They hurried toward him, smoothing their hair and giggling as they went. Excellent. That should occupy him long enough for me to find someone to check us in. The ego stroking wouldn't hurt either.

A nearby desk had a sign hanging above it with the word CONCIERGE written in fancy gold script. That looked like a good place to start.

A short, stocky guy in his twenties with short-cropped blond hair sat behind the desk. He was talking on the phone as I approached.

"Yes," he was saying, "I understand that purple is your lucky color. I'd be happy to change all your linens from white to purple."

He hung up, jotted a note, and then looked up and smiled at me, revealing dimples. "How can I help you?" he asked.

I looked at his name tag. "Mr. Scavolo," I began.

"Mike, please," he said with a smile.

"Mike. I just arrived and need to check in."

"No problem," he said. "Reception is right over

there." He pointed to the row of desks.

"Well, yes, I know," I said. "It's just that I'm here with a VIP. Justin Carraway?"

Mike nodded. "Yes, of course. We've been expecting Mr. Carraway and the film crew."

"I know this sounds weird, but I think he's upset that no one here has greeted him."

"I'll take care of that immediately." Mike picked up a phone, and in an instant a valet and a woman were at my side.

I led them over to Justin. He was signing autographs for the girls. Frank stood a few feet away, all of the luggage at his feet.

I smirked. Frank wasn't giving Justin space. Nope. My brother was avoiding the girls. He's like that. Pretty girls show up on the scene and Frank just gets tongue-tied and dorky.

The valet loaded the bags onto a cart as the woman stepped forward. "Mr. Carraway, welcome to the Pharaoh's Delight. My name is Amy Gloucester, and I'm your casino host. I'm also a huge fan."

Justin flashed Amy his thousand-watt smile. He was obviously feeling better.

"You're all checked in," Amy continued. "I'll be happy to take you to your rooms."

"Lead on!" said Justin. He waved good-bye to the girls, and we all followed Amy across the lobby, into an elevator, and up to the twentieth floor.

"We're not going to the penthouse?" Justin asked as we stepped off the elevator.

"You're booked into one of our most luxurious suites," Amy assured him.

"I thought I'd be in the penthouse!" Justin complained.

"The penthouses are reserved for the casino owner or special players," Amy explained. I could tell she was trying to stay patient. "You won't be gambling while you're here."

She slid a key card through the electronic reader and opened the door.

"How do you know I won't be playing?" Justin demanded.

"You're underage," said Amy. "We can't allow you to play. Now let me show you some of the amenities—"

"My film company dropped a lot of coin to shoot here," Justin snapped. "We could just pick up and move over to the Paradise if we're not happy here."

Luckily for Amy, a knock at the door interrupted Justin's growing tantrum. I hurried to open it and was relieved when Rick Ortiz and Sydney walked into the room.

"Excellent room, man," Rick said. "Look! The new SuperStation console."

He flopped onto one of the three sofas, flicked on the enormous flat-screen, and punched some buttons. A menu of twenty games popped onto the screen.

"I was treated so much better in Las Vegas," Justin grumbled. "They put me in a penthouse."

"They have the new Crusher game," I said, hoping to diffuse the situation. I joined Rick on the sofa and scrolled through the menu. "And Rock On."

"Check out the kitchen," Frank added, trying to help out. "The fridge is totally stocked."

"There is also twenty-four-hour room service available," said Amy.

"This suite is *sweet*!" I said.

"You're easily impressed," Justin said. "This is nothing to me. I had a personal chef on call to come and cook in my room in the penthouse at Piper's. And at the Versailles, I had access to a lap pool *in* my suite."

For a guy who wasn't a professional gambler, Justin had stayed at a lot of hotels in Las Vegas, I thought.

"This is unacceptable!" Justin shouted. "Absolutely unacceptable!"

FRANK

5

Mission: The Sequel

The Justin volcano was getting ready to erupt.

"Justin, I think—," Sydney began.

"I don't care what you think," Justin snapped. "Your job is to care what *I* think!"

Sydney slipped an arm into Amy's and walked her a few feet away from Justin. Amy pulled out a PDA and texted furiously. A few minutes later— while Justin pouted on the sofa—a short blond guy wearing a name tag walked in, followed by a uniformed bellman.

"Reinforcements," Joe whispered to me. "Mike Scavolo is the concierge, in charge of making sure guests are happy."

"If they're all like Justin, he has my sympathy."

"Mr. Carraway, it's a thrill to meet you," Mike said. "I'm so sorry for the mix-up. You were supposed to be in one of our penthouses, but somehow your reservation was confused with another guest's. We have another Carraway staying with us."

Amy raised an eyebrow at Mike. I could tell it was a lie, designed to soothe Justin's colossal ego.

"Good," said Justin, getting up. "Glad to hear it."

"Shall we show you to the penthouse?" Mike asked.

"About time," Justin said. "Hey, Frank and Joe, you should stay in this room. It impressed you guys." He turned to Mike again. "You'll take care of that, right?"

"Of course."

"I'm going to need a constant supply of Fruity Froots," Justin was saying as he followed Mike out of the suite. "But I only like the strawberry and pineapple flavors, so make sure the blueberry and grape ones are removed."

Rick rolled his eyes behind Justin's back. "Enjoy your digs," he said. He left the suite and I held up a hand to keep Joe from saying anything. I counted to ten, then grinned.

Joe leaped into the air, pumping his fist. "This room rocks!" he cheered.

We did a quick search of the entertainment unit and found the guitar-shaped consoles for Rock On. "So . . . want to play some tunes?" I asked.

"You're on!"

"Hey!" Joe shouted over the din of the game. "Did you hear something?"

I spun the dial to lower my volume. "Amp down," I said. He did.

There it was again—a knock.

I opened the door to find Rick holding a package. "This was waiting for you in the original room," he said, handing me the small padded envelope. "It must have been delivered before the room switch."

"Thanks," I said.

"Who sent it?" Joe asked.

I eyed the package. "Doesn't say."

Rick stood in the doorway, gazing enviously into the room.

"Wanna play Rock On?" I offered.

"Yeah!" Rick grinned, then stepped inside. He picked up the guitar I had been using and joined Joe in front of the screen.

I opened the envelope and found a CD. And two tiny walkie-talkies.

Whoops. I had just invited Rick in and now I was going to have to throw him out. This CD was from ATAC—and we needed to watch it right away.

"So what is it?" Joe asked, his eyes never leaving the screen.

"Oh, it's just a CD," I said.

Joe caught on. "I'm really beat," he announced, putting down his guitar. "I think that turbulence got to me more than I realized." He let out a big yawn.

Now I know for a fact that my brother has no future in show biz.

Rick gave Joe a puzzled look, then glanced at me. Finally he just stared down at his guitar. I felt bad. I didn't want Rick to think we were trying to get rid of him—even though that's exactly what we were doing.

"Uh, yeah, Joe. Why don't you go lie down," I said. I gave Rick what I hoped was a "meaningful" look, as if I was going to spill all once Joe was out of the room.

"Yeah, I'll go do that." Joe went into one of the huge bedrooms and shut the door.

I stepped in close to Rick and lowered my voice. "Right before you got here, he thought he was going to barf. He just didn't want you to know he couldn't handle a bumpy plane ride."

"I get it," Rick said, nodding his head. "I guess that means the roller coaster at the Steel Pier is out for him."

"Definitely," I agreed. "Maybe you should go. Just in case he has to make an express run for the bathroom."

"No prob," Rick said. "I'll catch up with you later."

I walked him to the door and slipped the DO NOT DISTURB sign on the outside doorknob. Then I knocked on the door to Joe's bedroom. "All clear," I said.

He flung it open. "There's a flat-screen in here, too," he announced. "And surround sound! There's even one in the bathroom."

"Well, pick a TV and let's watch this thing."

We settled in the living room.

"How did ATAC know we were in Atlantic City?" asked Joe.

I shrugged. "It's ATAC. They know stuff." I slipped the CD into the player.

Crashing guitar sounds blasted through the speakers, and pounding drums thumped a driving beat. Talk about quality. It sounded as if the instruments were in the room with us.

"Hey—those are the opening credits of Justin's movie *Z Force*," Joe said.

"Isn't this how our last mission CD started?" I said, confused.

"Wait. Something's different."

The movie continued playing, but now I could see that though the sound was choice, the film quality wasn't. It was grainy, jerky, and slightly out of focus.

"This looks as if it was shot by an amateur," Joe noted. He was as confused as I was.

The action sequence was over, and then the dialogue started. Justin spoke in English, but Chinese characters ran along the bottom of the screen.

"I can't believe the studios would release such bad copies to overseas markets," I said.

"I can't believe people actually pay to see this," said Joe. "It's giving me a headache."

The voice of our boss, Q, came through the speakers. *"Since you are already in Atlantic City,"* he said, *"we have a mission for you involving Justin, but one that is far bigger than just him."*

"Justin would be so hurt," Joe quipped. "To think there's something bigger than him."

"We want you to look into a bootleg DVD distribution ring operating out of Atlantic City. There's been a recent influx of DVDs starring Justin Carraway in the huge underground Chinese market. With Justin's worldwide popularity, he's a natural target. Everything from his films to his TV guest appearances to the old TV shows."

An old sitcom appeared on-screen, with Chinese characters scrolling along the bottom.

"*Five Times Five!*" Joe exclaimed. "Justin's first TV show."

An ultra-cute little boy ran into the living room, holding a puppy. He looked around, then put the puppy in a hat that was sitting conveniently on the sofa. The studio audience let out a canned "Awwww."

"Do you think that's Justin or Ryan?" I asked.

"Couldn't say," Joe said. "I *still* have trouble telling them apart."

"*As in the United States,*" Q continued, "*much of the bootlegging is done by organized crime syndicates who are often involved in other illegal activities. Atlantic City is new territory for them.*"

Five Times Five vanished, and another action flick appeared. This looked much more professional. In fact, it looked exactly like the original, except for the Chinese subtitles.

"*There has been a change in the quality of the bootlegged DVDs,*" Q said. "*The cheap versions were often secretly filmed during a screening with a handheld camera. Now they seem to be using the originals, which means there are film industry insiders working with the illegal distribution.*

"*Illegal distribution costs the film industry nearly four billion dollars a year. In fact, ninety percent of the videos and DVDs on sale in China are bootlegs.*"

Joe let out a low whistle. "That's a chunk of change.

No wonder they want this stopped."

Another movie scene appeared. Justin kissed his costar, Emily Slater, then turned and was riddled with bullets.

"Hey!" I said. "That's the scene they shot in Bayport. Last week!"

"How did the bootleggers get hold of that?" Joe wondered.

"There are already Internet boasts that the current film Justin is making will be available soon—and a few clips have even been circulated," Q said. *"There are promises that* Hong Kong Challenge, *the movie about to premiere in New York, will be available before it opens. This means they must be working with someone involved with the current film. This puts you in a good position to identify the inside source.*

"But be careful," Q warned. *"These are dangerous criminals. They're probably involved in illegal gambling, drugs, and extortion. There's a lot of money at stake.*

"Casinos are off-limits to anyone under twenty-one, other than the area being used in the film. Therefore we are providing you with doctored identification."

I rummaged in the envelope and pulled them out.

"Happy birthday," I told Joe as I handed him his ID. "You just turned twenty-one."

"These IDs are not to be abused," Q continued. *"We trust you to use them wisely."*

The CD did its usual self-destruct. Now all that showed on the flat-screen was a martial arts video with cheesy music. I turned it off.

"Looks like there was a big difference in the way the bootlegs used to look and what they're selling now," I said.

"Well, it helps if you've got an insider."

"So where do we start?" I asked. "Do we try to find the organized crime gang working out of the casinos? Or do we go after the industry insider with motive and opportunity?"

Joe thought for a moment, then turned to me. I knew exactly what he was thinking.

"Both!" we chimed in unison.

Dragon's Touch

"**R**eady to roll?" I asked Frank.

"Am I going to have to suffer through constant gambling puns?" Frank asked as we left the suite.

"If that's how the cards fall," I replied. He swatted at me, but I ducked easily out of reach. "Slowing up there, bro," I said. "Getting old?"

We took the express elevator down to the lobby, then headed for the casino floor.

"So where should we begin?" I asked. I stared at the football field–size casino floor, filled with row after row after row of whirring, ringing, blinking, and clanking slot machines. Even the ones that didn't have people sitting in front of them were chiming and flashing.

"We should get the lay of the land," Frank suggested. "We'll keep our eyes open once the crew arrives to try to figure out who the insider is. But it will help if we already have some potential crime syndicate suspects."

"I know the perfect place to start." I nodded my head toward the concierge desk. A woman in gold stretchy pants and a long, flowing top stood talking to Mike Scavolo.

As we approached the concierge desk, I could hear what the woman was saying. "Mitzi has never been so insulted. This is completely unacceptable."

"I'm terribly sorry," Mike said. His expression was totally concerned. "Please allow us to make it up to you. And to Mitzi."

"So you will make the spa appointment?" the woman demanded.

"I will not only make the appointment," Mike assured her, "it will be an in-room treatment. And, of course, it will be on the house."

"Well," the woman said. "That's better."

She whirled on her gold high heels, her long top swirling around her, and walked off.

"She seems a lot happier now," I commented.

"And I bet Mitzi will be too," Frank added.

"With a special spa treatment in her room."

Mike sighed. "It was the only way I could think of to keep the mangy thing out of the spa."

I gaped at Mike. He didn't strike me as such a rude dude.

Mike laughed at my expression. "Mitzi is a Chihuahua. Mrs. Milhausen tried to bring her into the spa for aromatherapy and a pedicure. When the owner refused, she went ballistic."

"Good save," I said with admiration.

The phone rang, and Mike held up a finger before answering it. "Yes, sir. Happy to arrange that." He hung up and immediately dialed a different phone. "Hi, Bobby. I'll need a limo in fifteen minutes to pick up Mr. Sullivan and his guest. Make sure there's a *Going Fast* DVD in the player with plenty of sparkling lemon-flavored water."

He clicked off and smiled at us. "Sorry about that."

"Listen," Frank said. "We're really sorry for the way Justin behaved earlier. The suite is amazing, and he shouldn't have dissed it like that."

I nodded. "We just want to make sure you don't think we think that's cool or anything."

Mike laughed. "Don't worry about it. It's nothing I haven't seen before. Besides, I knew what to expect. My brother Jimmy works in film production out in L.A. He's worked on a few of Justin's films. He warned—er, told me some stories."

Interesting. So our friendly concierge Mikey had film contacts and knows the ins and outs of

---

SUSPECT PROFILE

Name: Mike Scavolo

Hometown: Atlantic City, New Jersey

Physical description: Early twenties, 5'8", stocky, short-cropped blond hair.

Occupation: Concierge at the Pharaoh's Delight Casino Hotel

Background: Starting working in hotels as a teenager during the summers, worked his way up to concierge this year.

Suspicious behavior: Way too cheerful! Knows all the ins and outs of Atlantic City.

Suspected of: Being involved in a bootlegging scheme.

Motive: Money and connections.

Atlantic City. Did we already have a suspect?

"So we heard—," I started, but then the phone rang again.

"Sorry." Mike picked up, and agreed to arrange for seven concert tickets. "Yes, sir. I understand. Seven is your lucky number—each seat will have the number seven in it."

"Things are even crazier than usual," he explained as he hung up. "In addition to your film shooting here, there's a high-stakes poker tournament being hosted by this casino. There's also a Martial Arts Expo happening nearby."

"We heard about that," I said. "Justin is hosting."

"You must be filled to capacity," said Frank.

"And juggling a lot of personalities," I added.

Frank nodded. "From what I've seen so far, Justin isn't the only brat here."

"I would never call any of our guests brats," Mike said, his blue eyes twinkling.

"You must have intense security on hand," I said.

"We are definitely keeping on our toes," Mike agreed. "With all the money, the film equipment, and famous people around, all kinds of things could happen. And where there's money and gambling, there's often organized crime—"

Mike broke off abruptly, a light flush reddening

his skin. We'll have to add "organized crime" to his suspect profile. "So was there something specific you wanted to know about?" he asked.

I got it: It wouldn't look good for the hotel to even *mention* anything illegal!

"Yes," I said. "Can you tell us where the film set area is?"

"Of course!" Mike said overly enthusiastically. I guess he was relieved I didn't follow up on that organized crime comment. "Take a left at the elevators, go straight through the Fortune's Favor section—there's a big sign, you can't miss it. Pass the fountain and the ATM machines and hang a right. And if you get lost, there are plenty of hotel staff on the floor to help you."

"Thanks," I said, as the phone rang again.

"Yes," Mike said into the phone as we left, "I sure can arrange a helicopter tour. . . ."

We strolled through the casino floor in search of the set area. I kept my eyes peeled for potential suspects.

"Sensory overload," Frank complained after we'd made it about halfway through the huge Fortune's Favor section of slot machines. "This is giving me a headache."

"It's exciting," I argued. "Like a party always going on."

"A party where you could lose your shirt."

"Spoilsport."

We continued through the slots area and came to the table games. The casino floor was huge! And we weren't bothering with any of the corridors that branched off in different directions.

"Hey, check that out," said Frank.

Frank tipped his head toward an area called Dragon's Touch. Next to it was a noodle bar with a line of customers waiting to be served.

We wandered through the tables. These games were different from those being played on the central floor. I noticed one table had mostly women players, of all ages.

The table next to it was for something called pai gow poker.

"How is pai gow poker different from regular poker?" I asked.

"It's basically the same game they're playing with the tiles," a voice behind me said. "Just using cards."

I turned to see who was speaking. A young Chinese American man in his early twenties stood right behind me.

"Each person has two hands," he continued. "A standard five-card poker hand, and a two-card hand."

"Is it hard?" I asked.

"Learning to play is easy. Winning, that's another story." He laughed. "I'm Tom Huang."

"Joe Hardy," I said. "And this is my brother Frank."

"New players?" he asked.

"No. We're here with the film crew. There's a Justin Carraway movie shooting here."

"I know!" said Tom, beaming. "It helped me drum up business."

"What kind of business?" Frank asked.

"I work with one of the bus lines that runs between Atlantic City casinos and Chinatown in New York City. Atlantic City is a really popular destination."

"So what do you do?" I asked.

"I'm the tour guide. I greet the bus, help people find their rooms—you may have noticed these hotel casinos are pretty confusing."

"No joke," Frank said with a laugh.

"I tell anecdotes, I point out the whales—"

"I never heard of seeing whales off the Jersey shore," I said.

Tom laughed. "Not that kind of whale. That's what the casino workers call the guys who drop hundreds of thousands of dollars when they play. They're treated like royalty."

"Anyway," he went on, "this is my hometown, and I like showing it off. Did you know that the properties in the game Monopoly are all based on real Atlantic City streets?"

This guy could be a great source of info. He wouldn't have to put a squeaky-clean spin on things the way Mike had to for the hotel. "Would you give us your tour?"

"Sure!" Tom grinned. "On one condition."

"What's that?" Frank asked.

"Will you help me get a job with the film? I'd really love to get into the movie business."

Frank and I exchanged a doubtful look.

"*We* don't have any pull," I explained. "But we can introduce you to Rick Ortiz. He's the head PA. He might know if the film is hiring anyone local."

"That's good enough for me!" Tom said. "When do you want your tour?"

"How about now?" I offered.

"Sure! My group is going to be playing at these tables for a while. Where should we begin?"

"Right here," I suggested. If this section catered to Asian games and clientele, we might discover something about the Asian organized crime syndicate–Atlantic City connection.

"What do you want to know?" Tom asked.

"We've heard that sometimes organized crime gets involved in the casinos," said Frank, lowering his voice.

Tom leaned in close. "There *are* rumors—which I won't confirm or deny—that the infamous tongs have placed their members in the casinos."

"Tongs?" I repeated.

"Chinese gangs," Tom explained. "Not all tongs are criminal, but many criminals are part of tongs."

Jackpot! Just the kind of info we were looking for.

"Why would they move into the casinos?" I asked.

"Look around," Tom said, his eyebrows raised in disbelief. "There's millions of dollars changing hands here. Who wouldn't want in?"

He had a point.

"What started as a convenient way to launder money," he continued, "expanded to include all kinds of criminal activities. Supposedly some of the dealers and several players are linked to the dangerous crime syndicates."

"The casinos can't do anything about it?" Frank asked.

"You are a cheater!" someone shouted from a nearby table.

I glanced over. The person shouting was a handsome

Asian man in his early thirties. He wore a great-looking leather jacket, expensive jeans, and a tiny stud in his ear.

Everyone at the table looked shocked. A beautiful Asian woman stood behind the table, looking completely embarrassed.

"What's that about?" I asked.

"The man is Phillip Yu," Tom said, looking worried. "He's a high roller from L.A. He comes here about once a month, and also spends a lot of time in Vegas and Hong Kong. He travels with muscle. You don't want to get on his bad side."

"Noted," I said.

"And the dealer?" asked Frank.

"Jade Soon. She's a favorite among the wealthiest players."

I glanced over again.

There were no longer any players at Jade's table. Phillip was talking to her, but at a lower volume. From the look on Jade's face, he wasn't saying anything nice.

I'd seen enough. Muscle or no muscle, this was not okay with me.

I left Frank and Tom and stepped up to Phillip. "Okay, buddy," I said. "If you're not happy with the way the lady is dealing, why don't you just play somewhere else?"

Jade gave me a tiny smile. Then her eyes widened. I quickly understood why.

I was surrounded by several large, very intimidating men, all of them glaring at me.

Damsel in Distress

Leave it to my brother to get himself into a mess trying to rescue a damsel in distress. He did the right thing, though. Phillip was acting like a bully, and I didn't like it either.

I stepped up right beside him.

Suddenly there was a flurry of activity as the casino host, Amy Gloucester, two security men, and a fashionably dressed Asian woman appeared.

"Is there a problem, sir?" one of the security guys asked Phillip.

Before he could even answer, Amy jumped in. "May I arrange a private table for you and your friends?"

Phillip kept his eyes on Joe and me. "Yes," he

said, a grin snaking across his smooth face. "There is a problem."

"Oh, cut it out, Phillip," the trendy young woman said. She rolled her eyes. "If you have such a big problem with Jade, then why do you always seem to be at her table?"

A flicker of anger crossed Phillip's face, but it was gone by the time he turned to look at the pouting woman. "Min," he said, "I was only passing through the area."

Min put her hands on her hips. "You didn't have to stop and make a scene."

"You're the one making the scene now," Phillip countered.

Now the men who had seemed so threatening were trying not to smirk. They'd obviously seen Min and Phillip get into spats like this before.

Phillip threw up his hand. "Fine. Where do *you* want to go?"

Min tossed her long dark hair and turned to walk away. Phillip and his bodyguards followed, exchanging amused looks.

The hotel security guards and Amy disappeared into the crowd.

"Thank you so much," Jade said to us.

"Has he done this to you before?" I asked.

Jade nodded, her eyes cast down. "Any time he's

in town he finds an opportunity to insult me or to accuse me of something. I think he's trying to get me fired."

"Could he do that?" asked Joe.

"I hope not," she said. "I need this job. Thank you again." She hurried back behind her table, and several people sat down.

I turned to face Tom. "Could Phillip really get her fired?" I asked.

"I don't think so," Tom said. "Phillip only comes here about once a month. The big players adore Jade. And some of them are very connected, if you know what I mean."

"No," I said. "What do you mean?"

For the record, I knew exactly what he meant—that the players who sought out Jade were not just high rollers but linked to organized crime. But I wanted Tom to confirm that.

"Let's just say that they're the types you don't want to cross," Tom replied.

We left Dragon's Touch, passed the fountain, ignored the clanging and whirring machines, and finally came to a stop. There was no missing the casino area that was going to serve as the film set. Crew members bustled around setting up lights, dollies, and cameras. I spotted Rick wearing headphones and holding a clipboard.

As we approached, a security guard also holding a clipboard stopped us. "Names?"

"Frank and Joe Hardy," I said. "This is Tom Huang. He's with us."

The security guard scanned the list and nodded. "Go ahead."

"Things look hopping here," I said to Rick when we approached.

"It's getting done. Man, I wish Ryan were around. Or that I was with him on Isola."

"Isola?" I repeated.

"That's where Justin said Ryan went—Isola, in the Caribbean." Rick sighed.

"You might be in luck—we've got someone here who wants to help out," said Joe. "This is Tom Huang."

"My brother Jimmy Huang works for A-1 Production in L.A.," Tom said.

"Sure, I know Jimmy! He's a great film editor. I'm sure I'll be able to find you something here."

"Great!" Tom beamed. He gave Rick a card with his numbers. "I should get back to my bus group, but give me a ring when you need me. Thanks, guys, I owe you." He jogged away.

Rick glanced down at his clipboard and sighed again. He frowned.

"You okay?" I asked. He looked stressed. Actually,

the entire crew seemed . . . nervous. What could have them so on edge?

I scanned the area. I noticed a number of unfamiliar faces, but the crew was used to gawkers. That wouldn't explain the tense mood. My eyes landed on a heavy, middle-aged man with a serious expression. He caught my eye and immediately walked away.

Inside the marking tape stood a young woman with shoulder-length blond hair. I noticed some of the crew members glancing at her, then quickly averting their eyes.

"Check her out," I told Joe. "Why is everyone acting so weird around her?"

"I don't know." Joe studied her a moment. "But I'll go find out."

Joe and I strode up to her. "Hi," he said. "I'm Joe Hardy. This is my brother, Frank."

"Melody McLain." She gave us each a frosty once-over. From her expression, I could tell she didn't think much of us. "You're those boys from Bayport."

"That's right!" Joe said brightly. "How did you know?" He gave her a big smile. He probably thought he was being charming.

"Ryan sends me reports every day," she said. "*Sent* reports," she added sourly.

"You're with the film crew?" I asked. I hadn't seen her around before.

Melody sighed, as if speaking to us was tedious. "I'm the producer's assistant. I just flew out from L.A. Thanks to Ryan's vanishing act, I'm here to be the producer's eyes and ears. And with Justin, there's a lot to watch out for."

No wonder everyone on set was concerned. She was the big boss's spy!

"I can't believe Ryan just took off," she went on. "I thought he was better than that. But I guess he's just another spoiled brat, like most young celebrities. They're constantly rewarded for bad behavior. Screw something up, cost the producers thousands—even millions—and what happens? A little scolding and extra publicity. Everyone just loves a rebel. Hah! Not me."

"Uh, we're on your side," I offered. "We were with Justin—"

"Entourages just make it worse," she snapped at me. I actually flinched.

"The so-called friends offering temptations to goof off. No wonder people like Justin wind up with swollen egos. Not to mention the absurd salaries. For people who don't deserve it.

"There she is now." Melody abruptly turned and hurried toward Sydney, who was heading toward the set.

I couldn't hear what they were saying, but from the body language, it was unpleasant. Sydney did not like Melody, that much was clear.

The two women crossed their arms and glared at each other. Then Melody spun around and stormed away.

"Hi, Sydney," I said. "Does Melody McLain—"

"Where's Justin?" Sydney demanded.

"We thought he was in his suite," said Joe.

"Great," Sydney grumbled. "We've been here less than an hour and he's already off his leash. This could be a disaster!"

"What's the big deal?" Joe asked. "Isn't it Justin's day off?"

"He can get himself into all sorts of trouble if we don't keep tabs on him," she retorted. "I was hoping you two would help with that. And with that little snake Melody on set . . ."

"Yeah, she's something," I said. "We just got an earful."

Sydney sighed. "I'm sorry I came down so hard on you. I think I was just yelling at you the way I wished I could yell at Melody."

"We get it. We could see she was giving you a hard time."

"Listen, can you just go find Justin for me? I've got about a gazillion things to do since Ryan isn't around." Without even waiting for us to answer, she turned and walked off.

"But where—how—?" I called after her.

But she was already gone.

Boardwalk Boogie

"Where would a seventeen-year-old movie star go?" Frank wondered.

I gaped at him. Was he really that clueless? "Duh. Where there are girls," I said.

Frank looked at me. "Have you looked around? All the girls here are old enough to be his mom! Or his mom's mom!"

I scanned the area. He was right. Nearly all the women at the slots looked like retirees.

I snapped my fingers. "Outside. Remember, teens aren't allowed on the floor!"

"Good thinking!" said Frank. "There's a whole beach out there."

We walked over toward the doors, pushed them

open, and stepped onto the boardwalk.

"It's a lot nicer out here than in there," Frank said.

I couldn't really argue with that. Swimmers and surfers dotted the glimmering blue Atlantic Ocean. The pungent aroma of fried food mixed with suntan lotion. It was still early in the season, so the boardwalk wasn't too crowded. I took in a deep whiff of the salty ocean air. "You're right. This is cool."

"Which way should we go?"

I shaded my eyes. "We're almost at the end of the boardwalk here. Let's just start walking toward the other end and see what we can find."

"Sounds like a plan," Frank agreed.

"Well, I know how important plans are to you," I joked. "But first—" I jogged over to a bright white wooden booth and ordered a hot dog. Frank strolled over just as the guy in the booth handed me the foot-long.

"Nothing for me?" Frank asked.

I took a big bite. "Mmf f llumpf," I said.

Frank shook his head and ordered onion rings. Once he got his box of greasy goodness, we strolled along the boardwalk.

"There's a lot more to do than I realized," Frank said as we passed a mini-golf course.

"Somehow I don't see Justin as the putt-putt type," I commented.

Frank shrugged. "I hadn't seen him as a bowler, either, but he seemed to have fun." Then he winced. "Until he turned the Bowl-O-Rama into a Brawl-athon." He wiped grease off his chin. "Mom was right. Justin does tend to attract trouble."

"How much of that is really his fault, though?" I mused, eyeing the little stores selling souvenirs and saltwater taffy lining the boardwalk. "Sure, he can add to the problem, but a lot of the time he's just acting like a normal seventeen-year-old guy. It's the fans and the hangers-on that up the ante."

"You really do like your gambling terms, don't you?" said Frank. "Sorry, but going ballistic over not having a penthouse isn't exactly acting like a regular guy."

"Point taken," I said. "But how many regular dudes have their faces plastered all over town?" I pointed to a row of posters advertising the Martial Arts Expo. Justin's face beamed from the corner.

"Right. The Expo," Frank said. "Not only is he filming, he's got to host that event. He must be under a lot of pressure."

"Maybe he'd blow some steam in there." I headed toward an arcade full of video games. I peeked in the glass doors. No Justin.

"I don't see how Ryan does it," Frank admitted. "Being Justin's keeper isn't easy."

"That's probably why Ryan took off," I said.

"Check out that Ferris wheel," Frank said, pointing past the boardwalk.

"Steel Pier," I said. "The amusement park. I bet there are people our age there."

"I'd say the odds are with you." Frank grinned.

We picked up speed, but slowed down again when we saw a large crowd. They weren't lined up waiting to get into the amusement park. They were surrounding something—or someone. I had a sinking feeling I knew exactly who. Paparazzi were flashing cameras. People were taking pix with their cell phones.

"I think we found Justin," I said.

We jogged closer to the crowd. Now I could hear what people were shouting.

"Fight! Fight!"

InFANity

J oe and I pushed our way through the crowd, ready for anything.

I squeezed between two guys taking pictures and laughing. Sydney would not be happy if pictures of Justin fighting were published. But Justin wasn't brawling—it was two teenage girls!

"You keep away from Justin!" the tall, curly-haired blonde screamed.

"Hey! Hey!" I dashed in between them. "Calm down!"

"You can't tell us what to do!" the brunette yelled.

"Ladies, ladies! No need to fight," Justin said, stepping through the crowd, Joe beside him.

"There's enough of me to go around!"

The two girls gaped at Justin.

He clapped his hands. "Hey, everybody, listen up! How would you like to go ride the rides at Steel Pier? On me!"

The crowd cheered.

Justin pulled a wad of bills from his jeans pocket and led everyone over to the ticket booth. More cameras clicked. Sydney would be happy.

Justin handed me the money. "You take it from here," he said, walking over to the girls. I nodded to Joe, who followed him.

After paying for all the ticket books, I went and joined them. "Hey, Justin," I said. "Sydney is looking for you."

"Sorry, girls," Justin said. "Work calls."

"But you're Justin!" one girl whined. "You should be able to do whatever you want."

"Yeah, you can fire all those people, can't you?" the blonde added.

I was glad Melody wasn't here to witness this. These girls totally proved her point about fans turning stars' heads into homes for monster egos.

"But don't you want to see the next movie?" Justin said. "That can't happen if I don't go to work. Tell you what, why don't you give me your numbers and I'll call you when I'm free."

The girls scribbled their numbers and then giggled into their stuffed animals.

Justin turned to Joe and me. He clapped his hands together. "Come on, boys. Let's go make movie magic."

We walked away quickly. As we passed a trash container, Justin tossed the papers the girls had written their numbers on.

I shook my head. Justin had a way with girls— and also a way of breaking their hearts. That was one of the things he and his brother Ryan had argued about. Justin accused Ryan of just being jealous; that he'd act the same way given the chance.

We arrived at the boardwalk entrance of the casino-hotel and walked through the rows of slots and then past the tables. I noticed that several of the players at the tables said hello to Justin as he walked by. One even shouted out, "Hey, Carraway, hope your wallet is fat today!"

We strolled by a craps table, and I spotted that heavy man who'd been standing by the set earlier. He noticed Justin and gave him a very formal nod as a greeting. Justin just looked baffled. He didn't seem to know any of them. They were probably just responding to his fame.

A loud cheer at one of the card tables caught my attention. A guy in a cowboy hat had clearly just won a big hand.

Cowboy Hat gazed around the room to bask in the glory of his win. When he caught Justin's eye, his expression turned to shock.

Justin froze. He looked absolutely horrified.

JOE

10

Cowboy Hat

Justin spun and raced away. Cowboy Hat stood staring after Justin. His expression grew angry.

The card dealer said something, and Cowboy Hat turned slowly around to go back to the game.

"What was that about?" I asked.

"Let's find out."

We approached the table and stood behind Cowboy Hat. I tapped him on the shoulder.

He started, then turned and glared at me. "Yes?"

"I'm Joe Hardy and this is my brother, Frank. We were wondering—"

The heavy guy from the movie set stood up. It was like facing a mountain. "This table is for playing, not for talking," he rumbled. "You're breaking our concentration."

"When we play cards, we always talk," I said. "Isn't this a friendly game?"

"I'm sorry," the dealer said. He was a slight man, with gray streaks at his temples. "I cannot allow you to disturb my guests. Mr. Shin has already expressed his displeasure."

So the mountain's name was Mr. Shin. I saved it to my mental database.

"If you aren't playing," the dealer continued politely, "I must ask you to leave."

I pulled out my wallet. "That's what we're here for!" I threw down my ATAC ID and glanced at the dealer's name tag. "Mr. Wong," I said with a big smile, "I'd like to buy in."

Cowboy Hat and Mr. Shin looked amused. Mr. Wong simply nodded and said, "Our minimum is one thousand dollars at this table. How many chips would you like?"

I gaped at him, then quickly tried to cover. "Uh, well, you know . . . ," I fumbled as I shoved my wallet back into my pocket. "I'll have to come back later."

"Yeah, later," said Frank.

I let Frank pull me away. "So, big spender," he teased. "You get a raise in your allowance?"

"Ha, ha."

As we passed the concierge desk, Mike waved an envelope at us. "Can you give this to Justin?" he asked, handing me the envelope.

"Sure," I said. *If we find him, we will.*

"Let's check out his penthouse first," Frank suggested. "We don't want to show up on the set looking for him. Not with Sydney assuming we'd bring him back for her."

"Good plan." I didn't want to have to admit we couldn't produce him.

We rode the elevator to the top floor. It stopped, but it wouldn't open.

"Are we stuck?" I hit a button for another floor. We went down to 23, and the door slid open exactly the way it was supposed to. I hit Penthouse again. We rode back up. The door still didn't open.

"This is weird," Frank said, pressing the open button again.

"There's a phone here," I said. "Should we call downstairs and let them know the elevator is acting wonky?"

Frank shrugged. "Might as well try it."

I picked up the phone—and noticed it had three buttons: Front Desk, Alarm, Penthouse.

Guess which one I pressed.

Justin answered.

"Hey, it's Joe. We have some kind of letter or something for you."

"Who from?" Justin asked.

"No idea. Mike, the concierge, gave it to us."

"Hmm."

Frank gave me a questioning look, and I shook my head. Why didn't Justin just let us in?

"So . . . ?" I said.

The elevator doors slid open. Now I saw why you had to call to be allowed in—the elevator opened directly into the suite.

"Man, oh man," I said, stepping into the enormous, loftlike space. One wall was entirely glass, giving an amazing view of the ocean. "Some digs."

A grand piano stood in one corner, and one of the other walls was a flat-screen. Yes, the whole wall. The carpet was so thick there was a springy feeling each time I took a step. The sofas were as big as beds, and the low coffee table held several remotes. That meant tech toys were hidden away in the fancy furniture.

"The letter," Justin said impatiently. "Who is it from?"

"Doesn't say." I handed it to him.

Justin held the envelope as if it might bite him. Who did he think it was from? Cowboy Hat? Another stalker?

It didn't seem like he would open it. "Can we check out the place?" I asked.

"Sure," Justin said, still staring at the envelope.

Frank followed me down the hall. We peeked into the first door—the bathroom. It was as big as my bedroom, and the sink, the fixtures, even the toilet were solid gold.

"What kind of person needs a solid gold toilet?" I wondered.

We found a game room: pool table, another flat-screen with remotes, even an old-fashioned pinball machine set up and ready for action.

When we returned to the main room, Justin was still just standing there, frowning down at the envelope. Finally, as if he couldn't stand the suspense anymore, he ripped it open. He looked instantly relieved.

"Good news?" I asked.

He tossed the card and envelope onto the coffee table. "Just an invite to a party tonight. One of the high rollers here for the poker tournament."

"You going?" asked Frank.

"Nah," Justin said. "I want to prep for tomorrow's shoot. You guys should go."

"They'll know we're not you," I pointed out.

Justin shrugged. "It doesn't have my name on it or anything. Go."

• • •

"Why would a big poker player invite Justin to a party?" I asked as we stepped off the elevator. Even though this was also a penthouse, the elevator opened up without a phone call. Justin must have set his door to "lock" or something.

Frank shrugged. "He's a celebrity. They get invited to all sorts of things."

We handed our invitation to the security guard and moved into the room. This one had a different layout from Justin's. It had a balcony that ran along one side, and a hot tub, right in the middle of a sunken living room.

There were about twenty-five people there. I recognized some of the guests from the high-stakes tables. I was kind of surprised to see Mr. Wong, the dealer with the gray streaks. Did the players think that by including him they'd have better luck at his table? Or were they all friends, and hung out together?

I was even more surprised to see Melody, the grouchy producer's assistant. She stood alone in a corner, talking on her cell phone and looking worried.

I elbowed Frank, nodding toward Melody. "I'm going to find out what she's doing here."

"Good idea," Frank said. "I'll mingle and try to pick up some clues."

I pretended to follow one of the waiters. Just to make it look real, I grabbed a teeny tiny mini-burger off his tray. Why is fancy food so small? I lingered behind a large potted palm and strained to hear Melody's conversation.

"I promise I will get you the payment as soon as I can," I heard her saying. She sounded upset. "I'm so sorry. It's just not possible. I'm in Atlantic City on a job and I just can't do anything at the moment. As soon as I get back home, the check will be in the mail. I just need a little more time." She clicked off and slipped her phone into her purse. I quickly turned away so she wouldn't know I'd been eaves-dropping.

She let out a big sigh. Then she must have noticed me. Suddenly she was right beside me.

"What are you doing here?" she demanded.

"Uh, well, Justin was invited—"

"Justin." She sneered. "Tell me something. Does Justin have any concept of the real world? What he's paid for a single movie most people never see in a lifetime! Does he understand how hard it is for most people?"

She stalked away before I could come up with a response.

Boy, she really resented Justin's wealth. But if she hated movie stars and their crazy salaries, then she was really in the wrong business. And what was she doing at this party? Who had invited her?

I got my answer soon enough. She crossed right over to the mountainous Mr. Shin, who had been at the high-stakes tables where Mr. Wong dealt the cards.

They sat together on a velvet settee, heads together, talking very seriously. I could only assume he was the person who had invited her.

What other odd couples were here? I wondered. I saw Phillip Yu and his girlfriend Min standing out on the balcony. I quickly scanned the room, searching for Jade. Luckily, she wasn't there—otherwise there might have been fireworks.

"Mr. Swindon, I will take care of it immediately."

I knew that voice. I turned and saw Mike, the concierge. Mr. Swindon was a tall, thin man who didn't look happy. He was pointing at the hot tub in the center of the sunken living room.

"The water in this hot tub is supposed to match my wife's eyes," Mr. Swindon declared. A statuesque blond woman batted her eyelashes at Mike. "As you can see," Mr. Swindon went on, "her eyes are baby blue. This water is turquoise!"

"I am terribly sorry," Mike replied politely. "I will see to that right now."

Mike headed for the door, and I quickly caught up with him. "How do you do it?" I asked.

"Do what?" asked Mike.

"How can you stay so cheerful with all these crazy and ridiculous demands?"

"You get used to it," Mike said. "Besides, I have my own way to get revenge on each and every one of them." He winked.

Before I could ask him what he meant, there was a commotion at the door. It was Cowboy Hat again.

"I may not have an invitation, but I should be at this party!" he told the security guard.

"I'm sorry, my instructions are explicit," the guard said.

Cowboy Hat peered around the guard. "Hey, Wong!" he called out. The dealer glanced over, then looked away. "Tell this guy I'm okay!"

"I'm sorry, sir, you will need to leave," the security guard said. What he meant was, "If you don't get out of here, I'm getting my buddies to haul you out." Cowboy Hat knew it. He deflated and left.

"What's with that guy?" Frank asked, joining Mike and me.

"We get his type all the time," Mike explained. "A wannabe. He wishes he were a high roller and occasionally plays big. Mostly he loses bigger and not at a level that would qualify him as a serious high roller. Still, he's a guest here and has to be treated nicely." Mike sighed. "I'd better find him and smooth things over."

"Good luck," I called after him as he left.

Now if only we could get lucky and pick up some clues!

Retakes

They call New York "the city that never sleeps." I'd say Atlantic City could compete for that title. Here it was, six a.m., and there were already people sitting at the slots and the tables.

As we headed to the set, I worried that Justin would be a no-show—he wasn't exactly a morning person. Joe and I called his room, but there was no answer. With Melody McLain around, everyone was on their toes. It wouldn't help things if the star was late for the first day of shooting in the new location.

"This scene is supposed to be taking place at night," Joe grumbled. "So why are we up at the crack of dawn?"

Joe's not exactly a morning person either.

"Lots of movies shoot at weird times," I said. "Besides, without any windows it could be any time at all in here."

I waved at Tom Huang, who was beaming as he stood at the edge of the set.

"I guess Rick found something for you to do," I said.

Tom nodded. "Crowd control. Since the casino is still operating around us, he wanted to be sure he had enough people on hand to keep anything from interrupting the shoot."

I glanced around. This area was much less populated than the slot machines up front. That might be another reason the shoot started so early. Fewer people equaled fewer problems.

"Hey, Justin is already here," said Joe.

I spotted Justin talking seriously with the director.

"Maybe knowing Melody is here even has Justin on his best behavior," I said.

"He does look nervous," Joe commented. "He never seemed that way on-set in Bayport."

I shrugged. "The scene could be complicated."

A man with a dark tan, wearing a light-colored suit and a blue T-shirt, joined Justin and the director. They spoke for a moment, then Rick Ortiz led the man over to us.

"This is a good place to watch," Rick told him.

"Where do you want me?" Tom asked Rick.

"I'd like you to keep patrolling the area just outside the set," Rick said.

"You got it," said Tom with a sharp nod.

Rick listened to something in his headset. "Roger that," he said into his mike. "They're going to get started in a few minutes," he told us. "Tom, start your patrol. Frank, Joe, hang with Slick."

"Slick?" I repeated.

"My real name is John Slickstein," he said. "But everyone calls me Slick."

I recognized the name. He was Justin's manager, the man who made him famous and ended Ryan's acting career. We introduced ourselves, but it turned out he'd heard of us, too.

"Thanks for getting that wacko from Cleen Teens arrested," he said. He let out a big yawn. "Sorry. Flew in on the red-eye, so it's three a.m. for me. I'm going to try to find some coffee."

The director got into her position by the camera and monitor. She nodded at Rick. "Time for our first shot of the day," Rick announced. "Let's do it just like we rehearsed it."

Justin cleared his throat several times. "Can I get some water?" he asked. One of the assistants brought him a bottle of water. Justin chugged it, then handed it back to the assistant. He swallowed a few times, then did some stretches and shook his hands out.

"Does he seem nervous to you?" Joe asked in a whisper.

"Definitely," I said.

"Rolling!" shouted a man next to the director. I figured he was the assistant director.

Rick stepped in front of the camera with his clapboard. "Scene thirty-five, take one," he called.

"Cue extras!" the assistant director said.

Several men and women in fancy outfits started acting like they were gambling at the tables in the background.

"And . . . ," the director said. "Action!"

Justin strode into the scene as cameras dollied around him. He flipped over some cards on the tables he passed, smiling at the players. He tossed some chips onto a roulette table, then came to a stop at a table for craps.

Justin rubbed his hands together, picked up a pair of dice, and held them up to one of the extras to have her blow on them for good luck.

"Luck," he said. "Is it something we're born with or something we make?"

"He's really done his homework," I whispered to Joe.

The scene continued, and Justin didn't flub once.

"Cut!" the director called. "Good work, everyone. Hold positions."

She studied the footage on the monitor, then frowned. She talked quietly to the assistant director. He nodded, also looking serious.

"Okay, back to the beginning," the assistant director said. "We'll shoot the whole thing again."

Justin looked surprised, then nervous again. "Did I do something wrong?" he asked.

"No," the director said. "I just want another take."

Justin's brow furrowed; then he went back to his starting position.

By the time they shot four more takes, everyone was starting to get antsy. Especially Justin. But rather than having a fit, he seemed to become more and more worried.

"Break time!" Rick announced. "We're taking ten."

We went over to Justin, who was talking to the director. Slick had joined them.

"Why do we keep shooting the same thing?" Justin asked.

The director shrugged. "It's just off. I'm not seeing the same Justin sparkle I had in the footage we shot in Bayport. I don't know why it's not there, but I need you to get it back."

She went over to the food table and grabbed a doughnut.

"So, what's up, kid?" asked Slick. "You okay?"

"I'm fine," Justin grumbled.

"Tired?" Slick pressed. "Hungry? Whatever you need, kid, let me know. Anything to help you turn in a stellar performance. Justin Carraway pizzazz. That's what sells the tickets."

"I know that," Justin snapped. "I guess I just don't feel like sparkling today."

Slick's expression grew concerned. "Level with me, kiddo. Is it because of Ryan?"

Justin looked startled. "Is what because of Ryan?"

"Are you off your game because your other half isn't around? Look, *you're* the star," said Slick. "Don't let your brother's disappearing act spoil things for you. I could wring his neck. You're the one with the magic."

"He needed a break!" Justin snapped. "Maybe I do too."

Slick's eyes narrowed. "There *is* something different about you today." His expression grew concerned. "Is it this place? Is the, er, *environment* distracting?"

Justin's jaw set. "Right now, *you're* distracting me." He spun around and stormed away.

Slick watched him vanish into the now crowded casino floor. "I don't have a good feeling about this," he muttered.

"Is there something we can do to help?" I asked.

Slick looked at me as if he'd just realized we were standing there. "Nah, this is just Justin being Justin. I'd better go get him before he wanders off too far."

I felt for Justin. Everyone's jobs depended on him turning in a good performance. It must be rough having all that on your shoulders.

I could relate. On a mission, if we messed up, someone could wind up dead. But no one was watching our every move, just waiting for us to fail. And I had Joe. That made it a lot easier to deal with the intensity.

Could Ryan be the secret ingredient in Justin's megasuccess? Ryan took care of him in so many ways—from getting him to laugh to finding him the perfect milkshake. But who did that for Ryan? Justin may have the pressure of turning in A1 performances, but to me Ryan had the much harder job, with way fewer rewards.

Slick hurried in the direction Justin had taken, but slowed when he passed high roller Phillip Yu at one of the poker tables. He stopped and spoke to Phillip.

"How do those two know each other?" Joe wondered.

"Good question," I said.

Rick joined us. "Justin usually doesn't have to do this many takes."

"Could be because of Melody McLain," I pointed out. "Everyone seems pretty anxious."

"True," said Rick. "I can't believe I'm saying this about Justin, but do you think you can get him to be a little less pro and a little more loose?"

"That would be Joe's area," I said. "He's good at being a bad influence."

"Ha, ha." Joe smirked. "One other thing, though. Slick asked Justin if being in Atlantic City was too 'distracting' for him. What did that mean?"

Rick glanced around to be sure no one could overhear him. "During a shoot in Vegas, Justin got into high-stakes poker games," he said, his voice low.

"But he's underage," I said.

Rick shrugged. "With his money, people are happy to look the other way. Besides, he can be pretty hard to say no to."

"Yeah, I've seen that Justin phenomenon," I said.

"As far as I can tell," said Joe, "Justin hasn't gambled at all. He actually seems to be avoiding the casino floor and the players."

I nodded. "He skipped that high-rollers party last night."

"It does explain why he was invited," Joe said. "He must have played with them."

"I'm just relieved Justin isn't up to his old tricks," Rick said.

"You can't tell me what to do!" a voice shouted.

My head whipped around, and I saw Tom trying to keep Cowboy Hat behind the lines marking the set.

"Sheesh," Joe said. "That guy tried to crash the party last night. Now he's trying to get onto the film set."

"I have to see Justin. And you can't stop me!" Cowboy Hat shouted.

Suddenly Slick raced over. "Keep that loon away from Justin!"

If Slick was afraid of Cowboy Hat getting to Justin, he probably had a good reason.

We dashed over to help. I charged up beside Slick . . .

. . . just as Cowboy Hat threw a punch!

The Whale and the Piranha

My brother ducked and grabbed Cowboy Hat's wrist.

I grabbed his other arm. Frank clutched Cowboy Hat's wrist tight and twisted his arm around behind the man's back.

Cowboy Hat squirmed and wriggled. "Let go of me!" he shouted. "I'll report you for assault!"

"Back atcha," I said. "You're the one throwing punches."

A casino security officer stepped up to us. "Mr. Ziziska, I'm afraid I have to ask you to leave the area."

"Keep him away from Justin and this film set!" Slick ordered. "If we have to, we'll get a restraining order!"

"It's all your fault!" Cowboy Hat—Mr. Ziziska—shouted at Slick.

"Gentlemen, please," the security guard said. "You are disturbing the guests."

I looked around. People were crowding in, trying to see what all the fuss was about. I was trying to figure out the same thing. Slick and Ziziska obviously had history—bad history.

"Get these kids off me!" Ziziska yelled.

"I will if you leave with me," the security officer told Ziziska.

"I'm not the one causing trouble," Ziziska muttered, but he was a lot more subdued now. Frank and I released him.

Ziziska gave us all one last glare, then went with the security guard.

"Who was that guy?" Frank asked Slick.

Slick scowled. "A bottom-feeding lowlife." He shook his head. "I'd better go find Justin. I think the director wants to start again."

Before Slick could move, Justin stalked onto the set.

"Justin—," Slick began, but Justin ignored him and strode over to the director. Slick shook his head and returned to the food table.

I glanced around while Justin and the director conferred. "I'm surprised Melody isn't here."

"Maybe she decided she'd rather gamble on the

slots than on Justin," Frank said. "The director thinks his performance isn't as strong as it should be. Could be he's losing that . . . what did Aunt T call it? Oh yeah, *charisma*."

"If that goes, so does the whole Justin Carraway movie star machine." I let out a low whistle. "No wonder everyone's tense."

"Quiet on the set!" Tom Huang called out. Then he grinned. I could tell he was excited to be working on a real movie.

"While they set up again, let's check out the casino," I suggested.

"Good thinking," said Frank. "Why don't we start with Jade's area? That seemed to be where most of the high rollers hang out."

We wound our way through the long rows of slots until we found Dragon's Touch. The dealer with the gray streaks, Mr. Wong, grinned at us as we walked by. I think he still found it funny that we tried to play at his table. I tugged Frank's arm to slow him down.

"Check out Jade's table," I said.

"The players from the high-rollers party are all there," Frank said. "So? Tom told us the big guys like her."

"But look who's making a beeline for our friend Mr. Shin," I said.

"Melody McLain," said Frank. "They were cozy

at that party too." We watched Melody whisper something to Mr. Shin. He cashed out, then the two of them walked away.

"Let's follow them," Frank suggested.

"Great minds . . . ," I said.

The casino was still pretty sparsely populated, so we had to take care not to be noticed. We kept back a ways, but they were easy to keep track of—a very large man accompanied by a slim woman carrying a metal case.

"What do you think she's got?" I asked.

"Film footage?" Frank guessed. "Money? Could be anything."

I grabbed Frank and yanked him into a store selling souvenirs.

"Sudden need for saltwater taffy shaped like poker chips?" he asked.

"The whale and the piranha are behind that potted palm," I whispered.

I watched Frank's eyes flick to the corner. The Egyptian theme meant the corridors were decorated with exotic desert plants. A cluster of palms were camouflaging the rest rooms.

"We need to hear what they're saying." Frank and I strolled casually out of the store.

"I have your word," Melody was saying as we neared the trees.

"No one will see these. Not until the time is ready," Mr. Shin assured her.

She handed him the case, then ducked into the ladies' room. Probably to wash her hands after the dirty deal.

Frank and I spun around and pretended to be looking in the window of a fancy restaurant.

Mr. Shin walked off.

"What was that all about?" Frank asked.

"Should we follow him?" I asked. "See what he does with the case?"

"Well, we can't exactly follow Melody." Frank nodded toward the ladies' room.

We turned to follow Shin, but he was nowhere to be seen.

"He probably left the casino," I muttered. "To peddle his stolen film footage."

"We don't know that," Frank cautioned me. "Though it does look pretty suspicious."

"I'd like to get online," I said. "See what we can find out about Mr. Shin's companies."

"I want to find out more about that guy Ziziska,"

Physical description: Late twenties, slim, shoulder-length dark hair usually worn pulled back with a clip.

Occupation: Movie producer's assistant

Background: Started working at age sixteen and all through college; design major; MBA earned while on full scholarship

Suspicious behavior: Secret meetings with Mr. Shin; delivering mysterious items to him.

Suspected of: Being the insider giving original film footage to bootleggers.

Possible motives: Needs money and hates movie stars.

said Frank. "Try to figure out what is between him and Slick."

We went back to our amazing suite and pulled out our laptops.

I entered terms to try to learn more about Mr. Shin. "He has a manufacturing plant in L.A. And a number of businesses in China."

"Too bad we can't read Chinese," Frank muttered. All the sites about the foreign companies were written in Chinese characters.

"Try Ziziska," I said. "There can't be too many people with that name."

Frank typed the name. "Whoa!" he said, sitting up straight once the page loaded.

My eyes widened as I stared at the screen. "Ziziska is Justin and Ryan's father!"

SUSPECT PROFILE

Name: Mr. Shin

Hometown: Beijing, China

Physical description: In his fifties, nearly as round as he is tall.

Occupation: Successful businessman

Suspicious behavior: Seems awfully cozy with a movie insider for a guy who has businesses in China that have nothing to do with movies.

Suspected of: Distributing of bootleg films.

Possible motive: Money.

Family Matters

I stared at the search results, trying to wrap my brain around it.

"I guess they decided that 'Ziziska' just wasn't as movie-star as 'Carraway,'" Joe said.

"But why did Justin and Slick freak when they saw him?"

I clicked on several links until I found a newspaper article from four years ago. "This is a court case they were all involved in," I told Joe. I scanned the article quickly.

"Justin and Ryan had themselves declared emancipated minors," I read. "Until then, their father, Walter Ziziska, was their manager, and Slick was an employee in their production company."

"Why doesn't anyone else know this?" asked Joe. "This is the kind of thing the tabloids would have been all over."

I frowned. "Sydney—or someone like her—must have worked overtime keeping it as quiet as possible." I read more. "Also, it wasn't a jury trial. They filed paperwork and went before a judge, who gave a decision."

"How did Slick wind up as their manager?" Joe wondered.

"From what I can tell," I said, "when the court declared the twins emancipated, they fired Ziziska and Slick took over."

"That gives him a lot of control over a lot of money," Joe commented.

"And takes it all away from their dad. Firing your own father. Intense."

Joe nodded. "Can you imagine giving Dad a pink slip from ATAC? That's probably how Ziziska felt. He put his sons on the map and then he got the axe."

"I wonder if Slick had something to do with it," I suggested. "Those two clearly hate each other. And now Slick is rolling in it, getting a percentage of everything Justin makes."

"Let's go to the source and try to find out more."

We found Slick scarfing down doughnuts at the

food table. When he saw us, he gave us a guilty grin. "Caught me." He dusted powdered sugar from his jacket. "Everyone in L.A. is so diet conscious," Slick complained.

I decided to jump right in. "Justin seemed really upset to see his father."

Slick wasn't fazed at all. "Walter Ziziska is a snake."

"He doesn't seem to like you much either," said Joe.

"Of course not. I was the one who ratted him out."

"Ratted out what?"

Slick wadded up his napkin and tossed it down. "Thought you knew the whole story."

"We know you testified against him in the twins' case to be declared emancipated," I said, hoping that would lead him to tell us more.

"Walter Ziziska was stealing from his own sons. I caught him."

Joe's jaw dropped. "No way!"

"Way," Slick said. "He was supposed to be putting a big chunk of their earnings into a trust for them. Somehow the money wound up in his account instead."

"Did he go to jail?" I asked.

Slick shook his head. "That's what the kids'

lawyer wanted. I told the boys not to press charges. It was tough enough for them to cut him out of their lives. I thought it would just be too hard on them knowing they sent their father to jail."

I studied his face. So the slickster from Hollywood had a heart after all.

"Stealing wasn't even the worst of it," Slick went on. "He was pushing them too hard—sending them on auditions for things that they either weren't right for, or that would hurt them in the long run. He didn't care. He just saw dollar signs and went after them."

"You're more selective?" Joe asked.

Slick laughed. "You should see some of the junk Justin gets offered. It was true even back when Ryan was still acting. I think long-term. Ziziska thinks quick and easy. And only of himself."

Everything Slick was saying made a lot of sense. He seemed to truly care about Justin and Ryan.

"Like now," Slick continued. "Justin's performance is off. Don't know why. But I'm going to insist on a break. That'll cost me, keeping him out of work for a bit. But it's for his own good, and that's really what matters."

I was more and more impressed by Slick. I could tell Joe was too.

Slick frowned. "In a way, Justin takes after his dad.

Impulsive. Never thinking of the consequences. And they both have a thing for card games."

"Justin hasn't seemed tempted at all," I assured him.

"Do you think Ziziska came here because he knew about the movie?" asked Joe.

Slick's brow furrowed. "Anything's possible. But I *am* surprised he's staying at such an expensive place and playing at the tables with the high buy-in."

I had a sudden thought. Ziziska might be raking in the dough now because he was hooked in with the bootleggers. He certainly had access to the old material. He probably still had contacts in the production houses.

We had a new suspect.

SUSPECT PROFILE

Name: Walter Ziziska

Hometown: Orange County, California

Physical description: Around forty.

Occupation: Sponging off his sons. Now, who knows?

Suspicious behavior: Trying to get to Justin and playing above his means.

Suspected of: Working with the bootleggers.

Motive: Money, money, and more money.

"That's a wrap!" the assistant director finally shouted, back on-set. "Check with Rick for your call times tomorrow."

"I think that was better," Justin said as he jogged over to us.

"You did great," Slick told him, clapping a hand on Justin's shoulder. "Hardly any retakes this afternoon. Just do it again tomorrow and we're golden."

"My call time isn't until eleven p.m. tomorrow," Justin told us. "We're doing a night shoot at Steel Pier after it closes."

"That's good," said Slick. "You'll have a whole day to rest. Walk with me."

Justin's eyes flicked to Slick's face, then away. "I don't think so." He abruptly turned and walked away.

Slick looked baffled. I was too. He totally dissed Slick. What was up with that?

"Kids," Slick finally said. "Go figure." He pulled a cell out of his pocket. "Well, got calls to return, money to make." He strolled away. "Stevie, baby," he was saying as he rounded a row of slot machines. "What's the news?"

"What was that about?" Joe wondered.

"No idea. Maybe things aren't as cozy between Justin and Slick as Slick wants us to believe."

"What's your gut on Slick?" asked Joe.

I thought a moment. "He seems to care about Ryan and Justin. They're not just a meal ticket."

"Maybe, maybe not. Looks can be deceiving. Especially when there's so much money at stake. A good ATAC agent never takes anything at face value," Joe reminded me.

I nodded. "True. And I have a feeling he cares a little more about Justin than Ryan."

"That could cause even more tension between Justin and Ryan. The guy is practically a substitute dad. And as usual, Ryan gets the short end of the stick."

I cut him off. "Melody McLain approaching at ten o'clock."

Melody strode across the set, her face down. Just her presence put everyone back on guard, and the crew members packed up even more quickly.

Joe nodded. "Too many suspects around. Let's hit the beach and talk about what we know so far."

Sydney wasn't around, and Rick was busy with the crew, so after giving him a wave good-bye, we figured we were good to go. We made the hike through the casino again. I stopped when Joe grabbed my arm.

"Over by the fountain," he said.

I looked to the fountain. "So it changes color," I

said, not sure what had gotten his attention. "They do it with lights."

Joe rolled his eyes. "Not the water, doofus. The people standing next to it."

"The little old ladies?"

Joe stared at me, then back to the fountain. "Oh. Wrong angle."

He gripped my arms and switched positions with me. My jaw dropped.

"Phillip Yu and Slick?" I said.

"We saw them talking before," Joe reminded me.

"Yeah, but this is different. It's much more than tourists exchanging tips," I said, watching Slick grow more and more animated, and Phillip more and more intense.

"They seem to be getting into it," said Joe. "What could they be fighting about?"

I had a sudden thought. "Maybe Slick is afraid Phillip will drag Justin into a game."

"Do Phillip and Justin even know each other?" Joe asked.

"He *was* invited to that party. If Justin plays at that level, it's probably a pretty small circle."

"Should we go have a listen?" asked Joe, moving toward the fountain.

"Too late."

Slick spun around and stalked away. Phillip just smirked. Min appeared and linked her arm through his. They strolled away, casual as could be. Whatever Phillip and Slick were discussing, Phillip wasn't bothered at all.

The sun was already setting when we got outside. I took in a deep whiff of refreshing sea air. The boardwalk was a lot less crowded. We bought some pizza slices and sodas and walked along the weather-beaten boardwalk, looking for ramps down to the beach.

"If Tom Huang is right," Joe said, "and a number of the Asian players have connections to organized crime, we have several possibilities."

I nodded. "Starting with Tom Huang."

Joe stared at me. "You think *he* could be making bootlegs?"

"He has all the opportunity he needs," I said. "Not only does he know everyone in Atlantic City, his own brother has worked on Justin's films."

"I don't see it," said Joe.

"I don't either," I admitted. "But we can't rule him out."

SUSPECT PROFILE

Name: Tom Huang

Hometown: Atlantic City, New Jersey

<u>Physical description:</u> 5'9", short dark hair, Asian-American.

<u>Occupation:</u> Tour guide

<u>Background:</u> Went to film school and hopes to become a director.

<u>Suspicious behavior:</u> Knows everyone in Atlantic City, knows about the crime syndicate, and has connections to Justin's films.

<u>Suspected of:</u> Being either the insider or the bootlegger or both!

<u>Possible motive:</u> Money? It's expensive to try to make movies. Being a tour guide doesn't pay much.

"If we're going to consider Tom," Joe said, "let's not forget Mike Scavolo's on our list."

"He *does* know everyone in Atlantic City," I said. "If he wanted to sell things illegally, he'd have no trouble figuring out who to turn to. And he did say he had a way to get revenge on the hotel guests who drive him crazy." I frowned. "But the bootlegs turned up before Mike ever had to deal with Justin."

"Here's a crazy thought," said Joe. "What if Justin was selling his own DVDs? Or Ryan?"

That was an angle I hadn't thought of. "But why would they do that? They're already millionaires. At least," I corrected myself, "Justin is. And Ryan has the benefit of being his brother—and being on his payroll."

"I don't know," Joe admitted. "Just trying to think of possibilities. Justin does have that website, Justin Time, that sells memorabilia. Why would he need to do that?"

"Rich people like making money," I said. "They often have multiple businesses—fashion, real estate, lots of things. Let's stay focused on the more obvious suspects. There's that old rule: The simplest explanation is probably the right one."

"I'd buy Melody McLain before Tom or Mike," Joe said. We walked down a ramp to the sand.

I wished I'd been out on the water with the swimmers, boarders, and boaters rather than being cooped up inside the casino all day. *But we're not in Atlantic City to have a good time,* I reminded myself.

"Melody owes somebody money," Joe continued. "And she's awfully friendly with Mr. Shin."

"We don't know Mr. Shin is involved with anything illegal," I pointed out.

"We don't know that he's not," Joe argued. "We

have to start somewhere. And the two of them were acting very strangely, with that secretive exchange."

I nodded. "I wish we could have gotten a look into that case Melody gave him. But my money is on Walter Ziziska. He's tied in with the players—"

"Not as much as he'd like to be," Joe interrupted.

"Which gives him even more motive. After the twins cut him off, he must have needed money."

"From what Slick said, he also seemed to have come into some recently. Maybe because he started selling Justin's DVDs."

I frowned. "I wish I knew what Slick and Phillip were arguing about."

Joe thought for a moment. "We only know Slick's side of the story. We should add him to our list."

SUSPECT PROFILE

Name: John "Slick" Slickstein

Hometown: Malibu, California

Physical description: Late forties, six feet tall, overly whitened teeth, overly dark tan.

Occupation: Manager

Background: Worked for Justin's production company until he took over as the twins' manager.

"So basically we've got a bunch of folks who have access to Justin's films and possible contacts with the Chinese crime syndicates," Joe said. "But nothing more definite than that."

"Sounds about right," I said. "All we have are definite maybes."

SUSPECT PROFILE

Name: Phillip Yu

Hometown: Hong Kong

Physical description: Late twenties, about six feet tall, cool dresser.

Occupation: CEO of a bunch of companies. Inherited a lot of money.

Suspicious behavior: Knows a lot of film people; hothead, travels with muscle, rumors that he's "connected."

Suspected of: Being the DVD distributor in China.

Possible motive: Making even MORE money.

Joking Around

It was tough leaving the beach to head back into the noisy casino, with all the frayed nerves of the film crew. I guess I was starting to think more like Frank.

Yikes.

"We should probably try to hook up with Justin," I said to Frank. "Remember—we're supposed to keep an eye on him."

"Although I have to say, he's been a lot more responsible than he was in Bayport," Frank commented.

"You're right. Skipping the party, studying his lines. Like he's had a personality overhaul."

I stopped in front of a sandwich board, advertising events taking place in the casino.

"There's a comedy club here," I noted, reading the poster. "They're having an open mike night tonight."

"That could be fun. And safe," said Frank.

We took the elevator up to Justin's penthouse. This time we knew to pick up the phone to get in.

I punched the button and waited. And waited some more.

"No answer," I told Frank.

"Could he have gone out?"

"Hope not. That would make Rick and Sydney really nervous. Slick too."

"Try again," Frank told me. "That penthouse is huge. Maybe it's just taking him awhile to find the phone."

I hit the button again. "You'd think they'd at least have Muzak to listen to while we wait," I complained.

Someone picked up. "Who's there?" a strange voice asked.

"Uh, it's Joe Hardy. My brother Frank and I are looking for Justin." Who was answering Justin's phone? It didn't sound like anyone we'd met.

The elevator door slid open. Justin stood in the entryway, hanging up the phone.

"Was that you?" I asked, stepping into the suite. "It sure didn't sound like it."

Justin shrugged. "Don't want to let in just any-one."

"In that case, we're honored," Frank said. "I guess we really rate."

Justin smirked. "You just haven't gotten on my nerves yet."

"With Frank that'll happen in about"—I pretended to look at my watch—"oh, I'd say the next five minutes."

"Ha, ha," said Frank.

The movie playing on the TV behind Justin caught my eye. "Hey, that's you!" I said.

"It's *Hong Kong Challenge*," Justin said.

"The movie that's about to premiere in New York?"

"Yup. Slick brought me an advance copy," said Justin. "I like to see the movies before I go to the premiere. No big surprises that way."

Frank and I flopped onto one of the huge sofas. On the screen Justin was surrounded by a group of ninjas in an alley. "Looks like you're in trouble now," I told him.

Justin grinned. "Just wait."

Movie-Justin backed up against a wall. "I see you don't want to play nice," he said. "Okay. Don't say I didn't warn you."

The camera moved in on his face. His eyes grew

intense, and a sly smile crossed his face. "Time to kick it up a notch."

He let out a yell and executed a series of fast, intricate kicks and other martial arts moves. In no time flat he totalled the ninjas.

"Whoo!" I let out a cheer. "That was awesome!"

Justin grinned. "It did look pretty good."

"Time to kick it up a notch," I repeated. "I like it."

"They're going to use that line in the ads for the movie," Justin said. "They're even coming out with an action figure that says it."

"Ryan showed you how to do those moves?" I asked. "He knows his stuff."

Justin beamed. "Yep. He's a black belt."

I checked my watch again. It was getting close to show time. "We're going to check out the comedy club in the casino. Want to join us?"

"Nah, I think I'll just stay here," Justin answered. "Watch the flick. Study my lines."

"You're sure?" I asked. This was so not the Justin I had met in Bayport. Skipping a night of fun for what was basically homework?

"Why don't we meet up tomorrow morning?" Justin suggested. "Get in some surfing. It's way too easy to forget we're at the ocean!"

"I didn't notice any rental shops around on the

boardwalk," said Frank. "Where will we get the boards?"

Justin smiled. "I'm Justin Carraway. I want something, I get it."

The comedy club was packed.

Not surprisingly, hardly any of the high rollers were there. But some of the guests I'd noticed around the hotel were: Mrs. Milhausen had brought her little dog Mitzi with her. Mr. Swindon, the guy who wanted his pool tinted to match his wife's eyes, was laughing at the comedian up onstage.

Frank and I found a table near the back—ready for a quick escape if the jokes were really lame.

The emcee took the stage, applauding as the comedian put the mike back on the stand. "And now let's welcome our next comedian. Pharaoh's Delight's very own Mike Scavolo!"

My jaw dropped. Mike, the friendly concierge? Trying his hand at comedy?

"As many of you know," he said, "I'm the concierge here at this beautiful hotel and casino. The word 'concierge' comes from the French. It literally means 'the keeper of the keys.' I feel like a keeper, all right. A *zoo*keeper. Or maybe Keeper of the Keys to the Loony Bin."

Mike launched into a hilarious routine, poking

fun at all the crazy things guests asked him or asked him to do. Mrs. Milhausen was roaring with laughter, and so was Mr. Swindon.

So *this* was the "revenge" he was talking about!

"I think we can cross Mike off the suspect list," Frank said, clapping hard.

"All he's guilty of is a wicked sense of humor!" I agreed.

FRANK

15

Wipeout

The next morning was bright and beautiful. Perfect beach weather. I was psyched!

"Ready?" I asked Joe as I went out to the main room of our suite. "What's that getup?"

We hadn't expected to go surfing, so it's not like I had trunks with me. I opted for a pair of cut-off shorts and a tee.

But Joe had gone full surfer dude. Board shorts flapping around his knees, bright Hawaiian shirt, wraparound sunglasses, and flip-flops.

"Like it?" Joe asked, standing and turning in a circle. For me to admire, I suppose.

"Uh . . . cowabunga," I offered. "Did you bring that with you?"

116

"Just a little outfit I picked up this morning," said Joe. "Want to fit in."

"You got up early to go shopping?" I asked. "Justin isn't the only one with a personality makeover."

"We're going to be getting paychecks from the movie company," Joe explained. "I thought I'd splurge."

We met Justin in the lobby. Mike was there, smiling as usual. I wondered if this surfing expedition would wind up in one of his routines.

Outside there were three men in hotel uniforms, each carrying a board. I felt like a wimp, letting hotel workers carry the board down to the beach for me. But they wouldn't have it any other way.

Justin staked out a spot and we stopped. Not too many surfers were out; it was mostly Jet Skis and small motorboats. It was still early in the season, but the waves were calling to me!

"Ready to catch some waves?" Justin grinned.

"Let's kick it up a notch!" Joe shouted. I raced after him.

Yeow! The water was so cold it stung! But I knew I'd warm up once I got going.

I paddled my board out a ways and knelt on it, ready for the first wave. Justin and Joe paddled nearby.

"Here comes one!" Justin hollered.

I paddled the board to take the wave at the optimal angle. I could feel the pull of the swell sucking in water, building power.

At the perfect moment I sprang from kneeling to standing, planting my feet. I spread my arms for balance and rode just inside the curl, nearly all the way to shore.

Sweet!

I heard Joe and Justin whooping nearby. I turned and saw that their rides had taken them just a few feet behind me.

And there was another wave coming!

I paddled quickly to get into a good position. We'd floated far from our starting point. A boat zipped by, and the passengers waved as I straddled the board and paddled. They steered clear of us.

But another boat seemed to be heading right for us.

Justin had paddled out to catch the next wave. Deep in the swell, he couldn't see the motorboat on his tail. Riding ahead of the curl, he was picking up speed.

And so was the boat.

It was heading straight toward Justin!

Midnight Madness

"**J** ustin! Watch out!"

I saw the motorboat speeding right toward Justin. I couldn't see where Frank was.

The motorboat skimmed the break of the wave, riding up and over the white water as it curled over. Whoever was driving was using the water as a roller coaster. Was the boater trying to catch up to Justin?

Justin didn't hear me or see my frantic waving. He kept his balance on the board, obviously enjoying the ride.

I slipped off my board and into the cold water. I thought I'd make faster time swimming than paddling.

I stroked hard, warming up as I went. I kicked my feet, desperate to make it to Justin before the boat hit him—without getting mowed down by the boat myself!

I was only a few yards away when the boat whooshed around Justin, sending spray into the air. He yelped and fell off his board.

The boat sped away. But not before I got a look at the maniac driving it: Phillip Yu.

Frank swam up beside me. He must have ditched his surfboard too. "There's his board," he said, pointing to Justin's surfboard. "But where's Justin?"

As I swam closer to the board, I saw a bobbing blond head.

"Got him!" I shouted. I stroked over to him. "You okay?" I asked as I treaded water.

Justin nodded. "I think so."

He seemed fine, just a little winded. I knew from experience what spills from a board could be like.

"Let's head in," I suggested. "Frank's getting your board."

Justin didn't argue. We stood in the shallows, waiting for Frank.

"You're lucky that idiot didn't total you," I said.

"He came out of nowhere!" Justin exclaimed.

Frank came up to us, paddling on Justin's board. "I guess we should round up the others," he said.

I spotted Frank's board drifting toward the beach. Mine wasn't too far behind.

"It looked like Phillip Yu was aiming straight for you," I said.

Justin looked shocked. "Phillip Yu was driving the boat?"

Frank nodded. "Min was sitting right beside him."

"Do you have some kind of beef with Phillip?" I asked. "Would he deliberately want to hurt you? Or scare you?"

Justin went pale, then quickly recovered. "No, of course not! Look, it's no biggie. Probably just bad steering."

"We can report him to the coast guard," Frank offered.

"I don't want to make a big deal," said Justin. "It will just get Sydney upset." He shook his wet hair. "I bet there are going to be shots of me wiping out all over the Net!"

"If Phillip Yu is out to get you, embarrassing pix are the least of your worries," I told him. "Be straight with us. We've heard Phillip Yu is someone you don't want to cross. If you've gotten yourself into—"

"I said drop it," Justin snapped. "You don't know what you're talking about. I barely know the dude." He grabbed his board and stalked away.

"I guess our relaxing morning surfing is officially over," I said as we waded in closer toward our boards. "Who would know if there was anything up between Phillip and Justin?" I wondered.

"Rick?" Frank suggested. "Wasn't he with them in Vegas? He'd know if they'd met there."

"Rick will be at the shoot at Steel Pier," I said. "Let's ask him then."

We got back to the beach. The hotel employees were still standing there, waiting to carry the boards back. Justin was nowhere to be seen.

"Maybe we've made it onto his list of people he doesn't want to see," I said.

"That list seems to be growing daily," said Frank.

Steel Pier closed down each night at midnight. That was why the film was shooting so late. They wanted their night shots, but it also meant they weren't interfering with regular business.

It also meant an easier job of crowd control. Or so I thought.

"Don't these people sleep?" I asked as we approached the crowd surrounding the entrance.

Tom Huang was at the entrance, checking IDs.

"You look very official," I told him. "Nice headset. Very high tech."

Tom beamed. "This is the coolest gig I've ever had. Thanks, guys."

"Where's Rick?" Frank asked. "We should check in with him."

"He's inside by the Tilt-A-Whirl."

We went into the amusement park. The crew had already set up huge lights that blasted whitehot along the main drag of the park. The rides and attractions were cast in spooky shadows, making it hard to see what they were, other than looming shapes.

"I don't see Melody McLain anywhere," I said. "Must be past her bedtime."

Justin just nodded at us as he passed.

"Brr," I said to Frank. "I think we were just frozen out."

"What did *we* do to get on his bad side?" Frank wondered.

"Pressed too hard about Phillip Yu?" I guessed. "He's frozen out Rick and Slick, too."

We arrived at the area where the shoot would begin. "Snack time!" I said, heading toward the ever-present table. "Need to keep up my energy for the long night ahead."

Rick was already at the table, scarfing down candy and sipping coffee.

"Hey, do you know that poker player, Phillip Yu?" Frank asked, helping himself to a bagel and cream cheese.

"Sharp dresser? Pretty girlfriend?" said Rick.

"That's him." I made myself some instant hot chocolate. It might be June, but after midnight and right on the ocean it was chilly. "Any idea why Phillip should have it in for Justin?"

Rick snorted. "Justin gives all kinds of people all kinds of reasons to be mad. But Phillip? Who knows? I've seen him go off for no reason at all."

"During this shoot?" Frank asked.

"Nah, out in Vegas. He and Justin spent some time together there. You know . . . doing things Justin shouldn't be doing."

"Gotcha." I nodded.

"Could they have fought about a game?" asked Frank.

Rick shrugged. "With Phillip it could be anything." He frowned, listening to something on his headset. "Gotta get to work. The shot's ready. See you later."

There was something cool about being in the amusement park after hours. Like being part of a secret organization.

Oh right, I am.

In this scene Justin was being chased by some bad guys. The camera guys had their work cut out for them. They practiced moving the camera along a track several times while the director watched in the monitor and the assistant director talked to Justin.

After a few shots, Rick waved us over. "Justin isn't happy with the snack selection," he told us wearily. "He has requested that someone go get him all the salty items from the vending machines back at the hotel. Seems he has a favorite but can't remember what it's called."

Frank smirked. "Same old Justin."

"He's doing a good job, at least," Rick said. "We might actually wrap this up in just a few hours. Assuming we don't have any other surprises."

We jogged back to the hotel and loaded coins into the lobby vending machines. "Salty only," I reminded Frank as he hit the chocolate chip cookies selection.

"They're for me," he said. He opened the package and popped a cookie into his mouth. "Man, I feel for Ryan," he said, his mouth full. "Not being able to eat chocolate."

"Yeah, I forgot about that," I said, stuffing pretzels, nuts, potato chips, and crackers into my pockets. "I'd hate to be allergic to chocolate."

Suddenly Frank grabbed my arm, making me drop several packages. "Hey!" I protested. "Don't want to crush them."

"Leave them," Frank hissed. "We've got a new job. Following Melody McLain."

"What?" I looked up to see Melody walking quickly out one of the side doors, carrying another one of those metal cases.

"Wonder where she's going at this time of night?" I said.

"Only one way to find out," said Frank.

We raced out the door—and slammed into Melody. She must have stopped right outside the door.

She went sprawling, the case went flying, and lots of brightly colored plastic thingies fell out all over the street.

"You idiots!" she shrieked. "My Melody-Makers!"

She scrambled up and began to gather the contents of the case.

I bent down and picked one up. It was a bright purple hair clip that lit up when I squeezed it. I grabbed another one. A wristwatch that also lit up. And played a tune.

Not a DVD or CD among them.

A limo pulled to a stop. A uniformed driver stepped out and opened the door for Mr. Shin.

"Don't just stand there!" Melody yelled. "Help me pick these up!"

"Okay, okay!" Frank and I quickly gathered up the barrettes, watches, and other girly items and put them back into the case.

"What *are* these?" I asked.

Melody put her hands on her hips and glared. "Prototypes. Samples. My Melody-Makers designs."

"What happened?" asked Mr. Shin.

"These jerks knocked me over and everything fell out," she said. "I just hope none of them broke. I really do want you to like them."

"I liked the previous samples you showed me," Mr. Shin said. "I believe we might have a spot for you in Shin Manufacturing as a designer."

For the first time since I'd met her, Melody smiled. Not a strained grimace, but an actual grin.

"Can I just ask one question?" Frank said. "Why were you meeting so late at night?"

The smile vanished. Melody glared at him. "In case you haven't noticed, I have another job. I take my responsibilities very seriously. So I could only have these meetings on my own time."

"Let's continue this conversation somewhere more pleasant," Mr. Shin said. "I don't usually conduct business on Atlantic City side streets."

Melody took her case back from Frank. "Now I'll be able to pay my suppliers as soon as I get home," she was saying as she slid into the backseat of the limo.

Mr. Shin got in beside her and the car sped away.

"I guess we can scratch them off our list of suspects," I said.

"We'd better get the snacks to the set," Frank said. "Or Justin may have a meltdown."

We went back in and retrieved the snacks. Luckily, they were all exactly where I'd dropped them. This late at night there weren't too many guests wandering the lobby.

We hurried along the deserted streets. Atlantic City wasn't exactly a bustling town after dark. At least, not outside. The clubs, casinos, restaurants, and other venues were probably all packed, but here there wasn't a single soul out.

So my ears pricked up when I heard sounds up ahead.

"On your toes," I whispered to Frank. "Something's going on in that alley."

We slowed as we neared the mouth of the alley. I flattened myself against the wall; Frank did the same.

I recognized the sound: punches being traded. People were fighting in that alley!

I peered around the edge of the wall.

Tom Huang! In a fight with three martial artists!

Time to Kick It Up a Notch!

Three against one just doesn't sit right with me. "I say we even up the score," I told Joe.

He nodded, and we raced into the alley.

I flung myself onto the back of the nearest guy. Not exactly a slick ninja move, but effective. Startled, he stumbled and fell to the ground. I wasn't going to let him up, either. I sat on him. He squirmed, trying to throw me off, but I managed to keep him down.

Now that he had reinforcements, Tom began to hold his own with one of the attackers. Joe blocked a kick from the third guy and responded with a roundhouse of his own.

"Whoa!" I shouted. The guy I was sitting on

threw me to the ground. His foot came toward my face, but I quickly rolled away to avoid being smashed.

Suddenly all three attackers spun and fled from the alley. One yelled over his shoulder, "You remember this!"

"You okay?" I asked as I helped Tom up. His lip was bleeding, and he was probably going to have a black eye. He winced as he stood.

Tom nodded. Joe was nearby, bent over, hands on his knees, catching his breath. I was pretty winded too. I picked up the ATAC walkie-talkie that had fallen out of my pocket. I checked to be sure it still worked. It did.

Joe straightened up. "Who were those guys? They looked familiar to me."

"I—I don't know," Tom said, looking scared.

Funny thing is, I think it was Joe's question that scared him.

"Did you know them?" I asked. "Why did they go after you?"

"How should I know?" Tom protested. "They were trying to mug me. I didn't have enough in my wallet, I guess."

He stood there looking miserable, his lip bleeding, sweat dripping down his face. I decided not to push it. For now.

"Go take care of your face," I told him.

We walked Tom to his car. Once he drove off, Joe and I hurried back to the set. "Hope Justin hasn't been waiting all this time for his snacks," I said.

"I think most of mine were crushed in the fight."

"You don't buy Tom's story that it was just a random mugging, do you?"

"Not for a minute."

We jogged the rest of the way. I was really looking forward to hitting the sack. Between surfing, fighting, and all the running around we'd been doing, I was getting in a serious workout!

"Don't tell me . . . ," I said, slowing down.

"Doesn't anyone in this town sleep?" asked Joe.

Up ahead was an unwelcome sight. Walter Ziziska, aka Cowboy Hat, aka Justin and Ryan's father, was once again getting into it with Slick.

"I'll have the cops here in thirty seconds if you don't go—now!" Slick shouted.

"It's a free country! I can stand here if I want!" Ziziska retorted.

"I knew I should have gotten that restraining order," Slick said. "Get it through your thick skull. Justin won't talk to you. You can stand here all night and it's not going to happen!"

Slick turned and entered the park, gesturing

wildly as he spoke to one of the men working security.

"I'll have to hear it from Justin!" Ziziska shouted after Slick. Slick ignored him and vanished into the amusement park.

A security guard stood in the middle of the entryway. There was no way Ziziska was going to get past him.

"Here's our chance with Ziziska," I said.

Joe and I approached Ziziska. "He has no right to do that to you," Joe said.

"Keeping you from your own son," I said. I figured might as well get right to it.

"John Slickstein robbed me of everything," Ziziska complained. "He took all my money!"

Actually, it was Justin's money, but I wasn't going to point that out to him.

"So why are you trying to see Justin?" Joe asked. "We can get a message to him. But he'll want to know what it's all about."

Ziziska thought a moment. "Okay, here's the deal. There's a sweet game coming up, but I don't have the buy-in. If he could front me ten grand, I'll pay it back as soon as I hit it big."

I wanted to deck the guy. Slick was right—Ziziska viewed Justin as a walking ATM machine.

"Do you have anything you want to say to Ryan?"

I asked, wondering if maybe he'd show some feeling for his other son, since he wasn't trying to get anything from him.

"Why would I?" he scoffed. "That kid can't do me any good."

"We'll see what we can do," Joe said, obviously fighting back his own urge to deck the guy.

"If it works, I'll cut you in for a small percentage." He winked. "Like a finder's fee."

"Yeah, sure thing."

"Well, I've still got time to get in a few more hands at Mr. Wong's special table," Ziziska said, in a great mood now that we'd agreed to try to get him his cash. "I'm feeling lucky!"

He turned and sauntered away, whistling.

"What a creep!" I exploded.

"Slick is totally onto him," Joe said. "And now we are too. I'd say Ziziska is a viable suspect. He'd definitely sell out his own kids if it served his purposes."

"It's a good thing Slick got them away from him."

"And a good thing we got him away from the Pier. I think they're getting ready to wrap!"

"I'm ready to wrap," I admitted. "Glad there's no shooting tomorrow!"

JOE

"I love sleeping in," I said as I wandered out from my bedroom to the living room. Frank was already up and eating breakfast in front of the flat-screen.

"Room service?" I asked, flopping down beside him on the sofa.

Frank grinned. "It comes with the room, so why not?"

I plucked a piece of buttered toast from his plate and started munching. "What's up for today?"

"First thing, order you some breakfast so you don't eat mine."

"I'm not really hungry," I said, swiping a piece of bacon.

Frank pulled away his plate and stood up. He picked up one of the phones and ordered, then sat over at the table on the other side of the room.

"Mom always told us we were supposed to share," I said.

"So what's our plan?" Frank said, getting back to business. So Frank.

"Justin is appearing at that Martial Arts Expo tonight. The film crew is shooting exteriors and a few scenes with the guy playing the baddie."

Frank chewed thoughtfully. "We should try to talk to Tom again about that fight. And maybe get some more info on Walter Ziziska. See if he has ties to anyone who could be distributing those illegal DVDs in China."

"Sounds good. After I take a nap."

"You just got up," Frank pointed out.

"I'm weak with hunger because my mean big brother won't share," I said, stretching out on the sofa.

A meal, a shower, and two games of Crusher later we hit the casino floor. Walter Ziziska was on the buffet line, carbo-loading. Waffles, pancakes, *and* hash browns? I guess he was planning a poker chip-a-thon.

He brightened when he saw us. "Did you talk to him?" he asked eagerly.

Good morning to you, too, I thought.

"Not yet," said Frank. "But we will."

Ziziska nodded a few times. "Soon, right?"

"You bet," I assured him. Hey—that wasn't a lie. We *would* talk to Justin! Just not about Walter Ziziska.

Walter's eyes flicked away. The guy had no attention span. "Gotta go," he said. He dropped his tray on a nearby table and took off.

"Was it something I said?" I asked.

"No, it was someone he saw," said Frank. "Mr. Wong, the card dealer."

Frank was right. Ziziska and Wong were talking

over near the fountain. Wong kept looking around as if he was worried about being seen. He said something to Ziziska, and Ziziska whipped his head around. They loped away. To a more private setting, presumably.

"Wonder what that was about," I said.

"Mr. Wong was also at that high-rollers party," Frank noted. "He knows a lot of these guys as more than just a casino employee."

"Could he be Ziziska's Hong Kong connection?" I wondered.

Frank shrugged. "He keeps popping up in odd places. I think we should add him to the suspect list."

SUSPECT PROFILE

<u>Name</u>: Mr. Wong

<u>Hometown</u>: Hong Kong

<u>Physical description</u>: Slight man in his fifties. Gray streaks at the temples.

<u>Occupation</u>: Casino card dealer

<u>Background</u>: Arrested for minor thefts a number of years ago. Nothing found on his life in Hong Kong.

<u>Suspicious behavior</u>: Pals around with dubious types.

<u>Suspected of</u>: Being a Hong Kong connection.

<u>Possible motive</u>: Same old, same old: money!

I called Rick to see if he needed us for anything. "Nope," he said. "But ask Sydney. I know she's hustling to make sure everything goes smoothly with Justin's appearance tonight at the Martial Arts Expo."

I dialed Sydney. "Just checking in," I told her once she picked up.

"Darling boy," she gushed. "So kind. I've got Justin under lock and key, so I think all is well here."

"You've got our numbers," I told her. "Just give a holler if you need us."

"I've arranged tickets and backstage passes for you boys for the event," she added. "That's where I might really need you."

"Cool," I said, then hung up. "Looks like we've got the day off!"

"So what are we waiting for?" Frank grinned. "The Atlantic Ocean is just outside that door!"

"I think I still have sand in my ears," I said as we hurried along the boardwalk. We had spent a long day at the beach, soaking up rays, bodysurfing, and eating sugary beach food. We were having such a great time just chilling that now we had to hustle to be sure we weren't late for Justin's appearance.

"There's this thing called a shower," said Frank. "You might want to try using one."

I punched his arm. "I would have, but someone was hogging it."

Frank rolled his eyes. "This is the place," he said. He stopped in front of the arena. The door was flanked by enormous posters advertising the event, and a life-size cutout of Justin.

I heard laughter behind me. I turned to see Phillip and Min. Phillip was pointing at the poster and cracking up.

"What a joke," he said. "All this fuss over a guy who barely has a white belt. He shouldn't be the face of this expo."

"Whatever," said Min, clearly bored. "Let's just get out of this sun."

"Okay, baby," Phillip said. "I guess it's time for us to kick it up a notch." He laughed nastily and they went inside.

"We should go in too," Frank said. "See how things are going with Justin."

We picked up our tickets and backstage passes and found our way to the green room, the place set aside for performers to hang out backstage.

"Uh-oh," Frank said under his breath. "Slick and Justin are getting into it."

He was right. They were talking in whispers, but it was easy to see that they were having an argument. A very intense one.

Sydney stood off on the other side of the room looking worried. We went and joined her. "So . . . ," I said. "What's up?"

"You'd have to ask those two." She waved a gloved hand toward Slick and Justin. "Slick has banned me. He said he needed to talk to Justin in complete privacy."

I glanced back at them. What would Slick need to say to Justin that he didn't want anyone else to hear? It's not like Justin's reputation could be ruined with Sydney—she knows all his faults!

"You might as well get to your seats," she said. "Slick won't want you around either."

"If you're sure . . . ," said Frank. I could see he was dying to find out what the argument was about.

Sydney gave a sharp nod. "Sure. See you later."

We found our seats, right in the front row. If I leaned over enough, I could see into the wings. Justin stood there, fuming. Slick stood nearby, arms crossed.

"Looks like their fight isn't over," I said to Frank.

Before he could respond, a pounding rock beat started playing. Light beams shot out and swirled around the packed arena. A booming voice came over the megawatt speakers.

"Welcome to Boardwalk Hall, Atlantic City's premiere venue. Now, for the host who needs no introduction, we present Justin Carraway."

Justin charged onto the stage amid a roar from the crowd. He pumped his fist in the air, did a few wicked karate kicks and twirls, then stood at the microphone and grinned.

"Those moves looked totally pro," I said, impressed.

"Hello, everybody!" Justin said. "Just like you, I'm a total martial arts fan! And tonight you're going to see some of the greatest masters ever! These guys—and girls—have come from all over the world to impress you with their skill. But you're probably all wondering why I'm the person introducing all this. No, it's not because of my incredible good looks and star power!"

He made a face that told everyone that he was just kidding, and the crowd laughed. "No, it's because I'm starring in a film that's about to be released, called *Hong Kong Challenge*. So if you love what you see here tonight, turn out for my movie! You won't regret it! Let the show begin!"

A strobe started flashing, and the music amped up again. I wondered if Justin was going to stay to watch the show.

I leaned out to see if I could spot him in the wings. I only caught his back as he stormed by Slick and disappeared out the exit door. Slick shook his head; a moment later he also left the building.

"Justin just split," I told Frank. "Slick too. I'd hate to leave, but do you think we should follow them?"

Frank's eyes were on the stage. "Hang on," he said. "There's something about this group that seems familiar."

I looked to the stage. Three men dressed in suits came out onto the stage. "Cool costumes," I said. "They'll stand out by going for something different."

The three men took crouching stances. Then they went through a series of amazing leaps and midair jumps. "They look like they're flying!" I said.

One took center stage and the other two pretended to attack him. His hands and feet moved so quickly I could barely see them.

"Do they look familiar to you?" Frank pressed.

"I've never been to an expo like this. How would I have seen them?"

"Look at their faces," Frank insisted.

"No way!" I exclaimed, my eyes widening. "Those were the guys whaling on Tom last night!"

"But we've even seen them before that," Frank said. "Check out their number one fan. Third row, on the aisle."

I craned my neck to see who Frank was talking

about. My eyes bugged again. There was Phillip Yu applauding wildly. "That's the way to do it!" he shouted.

It all clicked. "They aren't just random muggers. They're Phillip Yu's muscle!"

"Why would they go after Tom?"

"Time we found out."

Phillip's bodyguards left the stage to thunderous applause. "Come on," said Frank.

We climbed over the people sitting in the row. "Let's go out the stage door," I suggested. "It's quicker, and we may also figure out where Justin and Slick went. We need to talk to them, too."

"Good idea."

We flashed our backstage passes to the security guard in front of the stage. He let us up the side stairs that led to the wings. We pushed through the exit door.

We found ourselves in an alley. "Which way?" I asked.

"I think they were shooting over near the lighthouse," I said. "Might as well start looking for Tom there. So we head thataway." He pointed down the alley.

In the dark I could make out garbage cans and doors that led to other buildings. I noticed a lump up ahead. "Slow down," I told Frank. "What's that?"

"It doesn't look like a trash bag," Frank said.

"More like a person. Stay alert," I said, as much to myself as to Frank.

We snuck up on the dark shape.

I gasped. It was Slick. And he looked seriously dead.

FRANK

18

Seriously Dead

I dropped down beside Slick. He wasn't breathing. I placed my ear on his chest. No heartbeat. I took his pulse. Nothing. He really was dead.

But he wasn't bleeding. What could have happened?

As Joe called the cops, I continued to examine Slick. I felt something hard on his chest. I carefully opened his jacket and pulled out a DVD.

"What's that?" Joe asked, clicking his phone shut.

"*Hong Kong Challenge*," I said, reading the title. "He brought one for Justin."

I handed it to Joe.

"Not this one," said Joe. He held it so I could read the back of it.

I took in a sharp breath. "Chinese characters."

"It's a bootleg. That movie hasn't been released yet. The studio would never sell DVDs before a movie has been in the theaters."

I rocked back onto my heels. "I hate to say this, but I think we just found our insider."

Joe looked down at the DVD and frowned. "Something . . . something else . . . ," he murmured.

"What?" I asked.

"Time to kick it up a notch."

"The big line from the movie," I said. "So?"

"No one has seen this film except studio people," Joe said, growing excited.

"And Justin," I reminded him. "And whoever made this illegal copy."

"None of the commercials have started airing, no trailers. And that toy isn't out yet either," Joe said, now pacing.

"Right." I wondered where he was going with this.

"So how did Phillip know that phrase? He said it when he was looking at Justin's poster for the expo!"

"You're right!" I exclaimed. "He'd only know it if he'd seen the film. And he'd only be able to do that if he was in on the bootleg scheme."

"I think we just cracked this case. Slick provides

the films and Phillip does the distribution," said Joe.

"But we still don't have proof," I pointed out. "Nothing that will put Phillip behind bars."

Sirens and flashing lights told me the cops had arrived. EMT workers raced to Slick. "His neck's been broken," one of the workers announced.

Joe and I looked at each other, both thinking the same thing. "Is it the kind of injury a black belt could inflict?" I asked.

The woman looked surprised. "Actually, yes."

"What can you kids tell us?" a detective asked, his notebook out.

We explained who Slick was, and Joe handed him the DVD. "We think this may have something to do with the murder. Bootleg DVDs."

"Interesting," the detective said. "Any idea who was in on it?"

"Not really," Joe said. "But you might want to look into this guy named Phillip Yu. We saw them arguing earlier."

We gave him our numbers, and the cops told us we could go. They were loading Slick onto a stretcher as we left the alley.

"Something's bothering me," said Joe. "Why would Phillip kill Slick if Slick was the supplier?" Joe asked.

"Maybe Slick wanted out. We know Phillip doesn't handle the word 'no' very well," I replied.

"You could be right. My money's on him. But we need evidence linking Phillip to the scheme and the murder. Or the cops can't pursue it."

"Let's try to get into Slick's room," I said. "I bet we'll find a paper trail leading to Phillip and his involvement. Even if we don't pin the murder on him, we'll break up the illegal ring."

We found out which room Slick was staying in when we arrived back at the hotel. As we rode up the elevator, we tried to figure out how to get inside.

"Maybe I can sweet-talk one of the housekeepers into letting us in," Joe suggested. "You know, let her think it's my room, charm her into letting me back in."

"Several problems with that," I said as the elevator door opened. "One: That would mean we'd have to time it perfectly so we arrived while they were cleaning rooms. Two: They'd have to have never seen Slick. Three: You'd have to actually be charming."

"You have a better idea?" Joe retorted.

"All the rooms have key cards," I said. "They usually give each person more than one."

"Maybe Justin has the other one," Joe reasoned. "Or Rick. Or Sydney."

"Man." I came to a full stop. "We're going to have to tell Justin that Slick is dead."

"And that the guy he trusted was stealing from him. Just like his low-life dad."

"I can't believe that Slick is no better than Ziziska." I shook my head. "Let's hold off on that bit. At least until we have real evidence. And he has a chance to deal with the news that Slick was murdered."

"I'm with you on that."

We rounded the corner and discovered we wouldn't need a strategy to get into the room. The door was wide open.

I held my arm out across Joe's chest to stop him. "Careful," I whispered. "Phillip could have sent his muscle for the exact same reason we're here. To find evidence of the bootleg ring. They could still be inside."

I pulled out my cell, ready to call 911. We tiptoed along the hallway. I didn't hear anything. I took a deep breath and cautiously peeked into the room.

The place looked ransacked. Justin stood in the middle of the mess.

"Justin!" I said.

He startled and whirled around. "Oh man, you guys scared me."

"What happened here?" Joe asked as he stepped over the threshold. "Slick doesn't strike me as the hotel-room-destroying type."

"I don't know. It was like this when I got here. We were going to meet up. The door was open, the room was like this, and Slick was nowhere to be found."

Justin's face grew concerned. "Do you think . . . Could there have been a break-in?"

"Sit down," I told him gently. "I've got really bad news for you."

Justin sank down on the bed, his face white. "What? Did something happen to Slick?"

"I'm afraid so," Joe said. I was glad he was backing me up. That I didn't have to break the news on my own. "He, well, he's dead."

Justin's mouth dropped open. Then he got a knowing look in his eyes. "Was it a heart attack?" he asked. "I told him he was pushing himself too hard. Eating all the wrong things . . ."

"No. He was murdered." I hated to state it so plainly, but I figured that was the best approach. How do you sugarcoat the fact that someone Justin had known most of his life had his neck broken in an alley? I was glad we'd decided to hold off on telling him about the bootlegs. He looked like he was going to be sick.

"Do the cops know who did it?" he asked, his voice a hoarse whisper.

I shook my head. "Nothing yet. But we saw him in a serious argument with Phillip Yu earlier."

He looked even sicker. "Phillip Yu?" Then he waved a hand at me. "If you don't mind, I just want to be alone right now."

"Understood." I hated leaving him there upset, but I also hated not being able to search for the evidence we needed.

"Thanks." Justin got up and went into the bathroom. I had a feeling he didn't want us to see him cry.

I took a look around the room. We couldn't spend any serious time searching—Justin was expecting us to leave immediately. But if I happened to spot something on my way to the door, what was the harm?

I could see from the way Joe was taking a strange circular route to the door that he was thinking the same thing. I bent down for a different view and noticed a piece of paper sticking out very slightly from under the window curtain. *That's a strange place to put a document,* I thought.

I quickly crossed the room, grabbed the sheet of paper, and shoved it into my pocket. Then Joe and I left, closing the door behind us.

"So what did you get?" Joe asked.

"Not sure," I said, pulling the paper from my pocket. I studied it a moment. "It's a spreadsheet of some kind. Hang on. Aren't these Justin movies?"

Joe peered at the list. "Yup. I recognize those titles. And those look like companies and cities. All in China."

"Dates, amounts." I looked at Joe. "I think we found some very important evidence."

"Too bad Phillip Yu's name isn't on it anywhere. All this proves is that the bootlegging existed. We still have to link this all to Phillip Yu."

"We need to pay a visit," I said. "To Tom Huang. He knows more than he's telling."

Recruit

Tom wasn't picking up his phone, so we got his address from Rick, then grabbed a cab to high-tail it over there.

We found ourselves in a nice-looking neighborhood a few miles from the boardwalk. We got out of the cab, checked the address again, then buzzed his apartment.

"Who's there?" Tom's voice crackled through the intercom.

"Joe and Frank Hardy," I said.

He buzzed us in, and we climbed to the fourth floor. He stood in his open doorway, waiting for us.

"Nice shiner," I commented as we stepped into his apartment.

Tom gingerly touched his black eye. "Did Rick send you? Do they need me for something?"

"Are you going somewhere?" Frank asked, eyeing the suitcase in the middle of the living room.

"Uh . . ."

Tom's red face clinched it for me. He might know more than he was telling, but he wasn't in on the scheme. He was just too bad a liar to be a criminal.

"Phillip Yu's men beat you up. Why?" I asked.

Tom stared at me. "How did you know who they were?"

"We've seen them before," said Frank. "They're the reason you're running?"

"I thought they'd back down!" Tom said. He sank onto a chair. "They said first me, then they'd go after some of my family in L.A."

"Why you?" I pressed.

"Phillip is a member of one of the Chinese gangs. He was trying to recruit me."

"And we all know Phillip doesn't like to be told no," I said.

"How much do you know about his activities?" Frank asked.

"Not much," said Tom. "Just rumors."

"Could he be involved in a bootleg scheme? Selling illegal copies of Justin's movies in China?" I asked.

"Sounds like the kind of thing Phillip would be into," Tom said.

"We think he and Justin know each other from gambling in Las Vegas," Frank told him. "Somehow Phillip got Slick to get him the originals to duplicate."

"If they played together," Tom said, "Phillip may have been able to get to people around him."

Frank pulled out the spreadsheet. "Do any of these companies belong to Phillip?"

Tom peered at the paper. "I recognize some of the names."

Frank looked at me. "I think we found ourselves a paper trail. At least one that can start a serious international investigation."

"Better move quickly," Tom warned. "If Phillip thinks he's going to be investigated, he won't be in town much longer. He has ways of finding things out."

"With his money, he could really disappear quickly!" I said.

Frank pulled out his cell and called the detective. After reminding him who we were, he said, "We found evidence that Phillip Yu is involved in the bootlegging that may have been the reason John Slickstein was murdered. Phillip's a serious flight risk." They spoke a few more minutes, then he told us that the cops were putting out an APB, covering the airport and the highways.

"You should be safe now," he told Tom. "Phillip is going to be too busy trying to save his butt to come after you."

We left and took a cab back to the hotel. "What next?" I asked.

"Let's try to find Phillip. Maybe he doesn't know yet that the cops are after him. We can try to stall him, prevent him from leaving."

Phillip wasn't on the casino floor so we hit the boardwalk, eyes peeled. There were still people out, even though it was now nearly midnight. Things were shutting down, though, and as each little shop closed, the boardwalk grew darker.

"Isn't that Justin?" Frank asked. "Just beyond the mini-golf?"

I peered into the dark. "You're right. He's talking on his cell."

"I wonder if he wants company," Frank said. "Or if he's still too upset."

Justin hung up, and we watched a little longer, trying to gauge his mood. Too tough to determine from this far away in the dark.

"Let's go join him," I said. "If he doesn't want to talk to us, he'll tell us. He has no trouble doing that."

Justin was on the move now, walking at a quick clip. In a few minutes he was joined by someone else.

Phillip Yu!

"Oh man," I said. "I hope Justin isn't planning to confront Phillip about Slick!"

"We have to get over there—fast!"

Frank and I took off, our feet pounding the boardwalk. People gave us dirty looks, but I didn't care. Justin was no match for Phillip.

Phillip must have seen us, because he abruptly turned and ran. We thundered up to Justin.

"What's the hurry?" Justin asked.

"You stay with Justin," Frank told me. "I'm going after Phillip."

"But—," I started to protest, but he had already taken off.

"Did you call Phillip and ask him to meet you?" I demanded.

"What? Of course not!" Justin said. "I called Ryan. I had to tell him about what happened to Slick."

"Of course," I said. I shouldn't be coming down so hard on him. He was dealing with a lot. "But why were you talking to Phillip?"

"I don't know. You told me he was a suspect, so when I saw him I, I guess I wanted to do something. For Slick."

"I understand," I told him. "But it's a good thing we caught up with you. Phillip is very dangerous." And I just let my brother go after him alone! "Listen, can I trust you to just go back to the penthouse? I need to help Frank."

"Uh, yeah, sure."

I didn't quite believe him, but what could I do? I couldn't let my brother face Phillip on his own.

But where were they? I charged along the now-deserted boardwalk. I didn't see them on the beach. Then I remembered the walkie-talkies provided by ATAC. I only hoped Frank remembered his.

I turned it on. I didn't want to risk revealing Frank's position to Phillip if he was in hiding. So I listened.

I smiled. From the crackle and ambient sound I knew Frank had turned on his, too.

Then I heard Frank whisper, "Steel Pier." Then I heard something else.

A gunshot!

A Fatal Gamble

I ducked just in time. A bullet whizzed by my face and ricocheted off the steel gates that normally kept out intruders. Intruders like Phillip Yu. And me.

After watching Phillip scale the gate and drop into the park, I did the same thing. Maybe that wasn't so smart. It was pitch-dark, and I didn't want to risk using my flashlight.

I had switched on the walkie-talkie as I chased Phillip. Now I wished I had mentioned to Joe that I was going to do that. I hoped he would try his and figure out where we were. There was no way we'd be seen from the boardwalk.

Bang! BANG!

I heard a soft thud behind me. *Please be Joe*, I thought.

"Your backup has arrived," Joe whispered. "Any idea where he is?"

"None," I admitted. "From the shots it seemed he was heading toward the water."

Joe and I crept through the park, keeping close to the rides. Open space was not our friend. We needed cover.

We ducked down below the platform of a carousel. We had almost made it all the way to the edge of the park. "Why would he come into the park?" Joe wondered. "He's trapped in here, just like we are."

Then I heard an unmistakable sound. A helicopter starting up.

"That's why he came here," I said. "The helipad!"

"If he takes off in that thing," Joe said, "no one will ever see him again."

No time to play it safe now! The helicopter's blades were spinning. The wind from the rotating blades blew trash and sand at us, and the roar of the blades was deafening. Joe and I kept our heads down and raced for the helicopter. I really hoped Phillip was alone. That way all of his concentration would be on flying the helicopter, and he wouldn't keep shooting at us.

"Lift-off!" Joe cried in dismay.

The helicopter was leaving the ground. I wasn't going to let Phillip get away.

I flung myself forward and grabbed one of the feet of the aircraft as it passed my face. I gripped the cold metal as the helicopter continued to rise.

Suddenly my shoulders burned and the pressure on my hands grew intense. Joe had jumped up and grabbed onto my ankles.

We were dangling tandem underneath a moving helicopter!

I winced, then gritted my teeth, willing myself to hang on, despite the added weight of my brother hanging below me.

"Hold on tight!" he shouted to me. "I'm going to climb!"

Despite the cold night ocean air, sweat poured down my face. Every fiber in my arm muscles burned. Joe inched his way up my body until he was able to reach over and grab one of the other helicopter feet.

He stretched out, and in an amazing move managed to grab a metal strut, then swing himself off me and over to the other leg.

All without knocking me into the churning Atlantic Ocean.

We were right below the opening into the copter.

These babies have no doors. I wanted to get inside, fast. I didn't know how much longer my strength would hold up.

Joe started swinging below the belly of the copter. Was he going to fall?

No! He was trying swing his legs up and over into the open doorway!

After three tries, he managed to get his legs inside.

He shimmied into the helicopter and vanished for a moment, then poked his head out.

"Give me your hand!" he shouted over the roar of the blades.

"What are you doing in here?" I heard Phillip shout from inside the copter.

I stretched as far as I could to reach Joe's hands. He lay flat on the helicopter floor. I didn't want to think about what would happen if Phillip left the controls at this moment.

I gripped Joe's wrist and he gripped mine—that's a safe hold. I tried to help him as best I could as he dragged me toward the opening.

The moment my chest reached the doorway I folded myself over the opening. He let go of my hand and grabbed my hips and tugged me the rest of the way in.

I stumbled as the helicopter lurched. Phillip was

trying to get us to fall out the open sides by twisting and turning the copter!

I grabbed Joe's shirt as he teetered dangerously toward the open doorway. Once I was sure he was steady I planted my hand and braced myself against the ceiling.

"Give up, Phillip!" I shouted. "The cops are onto you. You'll never get away!"

"You've ruined everything!" In a rage, Phillip leaped out of his seat and flung himself at me. The copter began spinning crazily, and the three of us fell to the floor.

"Joe!" I cried. "Grab the controls!"

Joe scrambled back up, then ducked back down as Phillip swung at him. I threw myself at Phillip's midsection.

"Oof!" He grunted and fell back down. I heard something clatter to the floor as I crouched and grabbed for him. He kicked sharply, knocking my chin hard. I stumbled backward as the copter changed direction again. It stopped its crazy spiral and straightened out.

Joe must have made it to the controls.

Now we just had to get Phillip under control.

Phillip was crouching now. The copter was too small to stand in. He looked like he was in a martial arts stance.

I knew I could never match Phillip's moves. I held up my hands. "This is crazy," I told him. "You can't win."

"I never lose!" Phillip sneered.

He took a quick glance over his shoulder. Then, in another one of his lightning moves, he leaped out of the helicopter!

"No!" I screamed. I stared down into the inky ocean. "He jumped!" I shouted to Joe. "Turn on the lights!"

Joe flicked on the headlights. I couldn't see Phillip anywhere. He must have gone under.

"He's gone," I told Joe. I leaned down and picked up the object that had fallen out of Phillip's pocket. A handheld organizer. I had a feeling it could contain very important information. I slipped it into my pocket.

"Why would he do that?" Joe asked. "Just jump?"

"Maybe he thought he could survive the fall. If he did, he might be able to survive long enough to be rescued. These waters are pretty well trafficked. As long as he wasn't rescued by cops, he might have gotten away."

"Phillip Yu was a gambler," said Joe, "but this was a gamble he lost."

"Let's get this baby grounded," I said, sliding wearily to the floor.

Hurricane!

t was a lot easier landing the helicopter than it was getting into it. By the time we returned it to the helipad, the cops had arrived.

"Phillip Yu was trying to escape because he knew that you were going to be able to prove he was involved in the illegal DVDs and Slick's murder," Frank explained to a police officer.

"But he jumped out of the helicopter," I added.

The cop nodded. "We'll get the coast guard to do a search, but I doubt we'll find him alive."

Frank started fumbling in his pocket. I wondered what he was looking for. But before he pulled out anything, Rick rushed up to us.

"I'm so glad I found you!" he said.

"How did you?" I asked.

He looked sheepish. "I don't know. I saw the cops and somehow figured you guys had to be involved. You seem to always be around when crazy things happen."

"Why were you looking for us?" Frank asked, changing the subject quickly.

"I was watching the news," said Rick. "The island where Ryan is staying has been devastated by a hurricane!"

"What?"

"I've been trying to reach him, but his cell isn't working."

"But Justin was just talking to him on his cell!" I said. "That's who he was talking to before he spotted Phillip."

"That's not possible," Rick said. "According to the news, the storm hit two days ago. There's been no service at all!"

"Listen," said Frank, "if Ryan is still on that island, we know people who can help."

"And if he's not?" Rick asked worriedly.

"We should track him down anyway," I said. "After all that's happened here, I'm sure Ryan would want to be back with Justin."

"That's true," Frank added. "After losing Slick, they need each other."

"We promise to do everything we can to find Ryan and bring him back."

I glanced at Frank. He seemed to agree that was exactly what we should do next. Which meant we had another mystery to solve.

FRANKLIN W. DIXON

THE HARDY BOYS

Undercover Brothers®

INVESTIGATE THESE TWO ADVENTUROUS MYSTERY TRILOGIES WITH AGENTS FRANK AND JOE HARDY!

#25 Double Trouble

#26 Double Down

#28 Galaxy X

#29 X-plosion

#27 Double Deception

#30 The X-Factor

From Aladdin
Published by Simon & Schuster

PENDRAGON

Bobby Pendragon is a seemingly normal fourteen-year-old boy. He has a family, a home, and a possible new girlfriend. But something happens to Bobby that changes his life forever.

HE IS CHOSEN TO DETERMINE
THE COURSE OF HUMAN EXISTENCE.

Pulled away from the comfort of his family and suburban home, Bobby is launched into the middle of an immense, interdimensional conflict. It's a journey of danger and discovery for Bobby, and his success or failure will do nothing less than determine the fate of the world. . . .

From Aladdin • Published by Simon & Schuster